The Tree of the Seventh Heaven

The TREE of the SEVENTH HEAVEN

MILTON HATOUM

TRANSLATED FROM THE PORTUGUESE
BY ELLEN WATSON

ATHENEUM • NEW YORK • 1994
Maxwell Macmillan Canada • Toronto
Maxwell Macmillan International
New York Oxford Singapore Sydney

Atheneum   Maxwell Macmillan Canada, Inc.
Macmillan Publishing Company   1200 Eglinton Avenue East
866 Third Avenue   Suite 200
New York, NY   10022 Don Mills, Ontario M3C 3N1

Macmillan Publishing Company is part of the Maxwell Communications
Group of Companies

Library of Congress Cataloging-in-Publication Data
Hatoum, Milton.
[Relato de um certo oriente. English]
The tree of the seventh heaven/Milton Hatoum: translated from the
Portuguese by Ellen Watson.
            p.   cm.
          ISBN 0-689-12165-2
              I. Title.
PQ9698.18.A86R413   1994
869.3—dc20   93-31148

Macmillan books are available at special discounts for bulk
purchases for sales promotions, premiums, fund-raising, or educational
use. For details, contact:
Special Sales Director
Macmillan Publishing Company
866 Third Avenue
New York, NY 10022

10 9 8 7 6 5 4 3 2 1

To the memory of Sada and Fadel,
to my parents,
and to Rita

The author and the translator gratefully acknowledge
Bruce Osborne in Brazil and Veronica Cavalcanti in
the United States for their generous
assistance in the preparation of this translation.

Shall memory restore
The steps and the shore,
The face and the meeting place . . . ?
W. H. AUDEN

The Tree of the
Seventh
Heaven

THE RETURN

I OPENED MY EYES to two looming faces, a woman and a child. They were motionless above me, and the cloudy morning's indecisive light seemed to be sending their bodies back to sleep or toward the weariness of a wakeful night. I had somehow mysteriously left the place where I'd chosen to bed down and ended up in a kind of grotto of plants, between the lamppost and the breezeway, that led to the back door. I was lying on the grass, huddled up because of the dew; my clothes felt damp on my skin and my hands were still resting on the curling pages of an open notebook where, half asleep, I'd scribbled my impressions of last night's flight. I remembered falling asleep staring at the contours of the locked and silent house, trying to visualize the profiles of the two stone lions under the mango trees across the street.

The woman edged closer and wordlessly used her foot to nudge away a rag doll that lay on the ground between my face and my knapsack; then she was still again, her gaze lost in the dark of the greenery, while the child grabbed the rag doll and zigzagged off toward the house. I was struggling to place the woman's face. I kept thinking she was linked to some intimate part of my childhood, but I saw no familiar feature, no sign that beckoned to the past. I told her who I was and when I had arrived, and asked her name.

"I am Anastácia's daughter and one of Emilie's goddaughters" was all she said.

She motioned for me to come inside. There was a room all ready for me and breakfast waiting. The air was thick with a strong aroma that immediately brought back the color, consistency, shape, and taste of those fruits we used to pull down from the trees encircling the patio at Emilie's house. Before going to the kitchen, I decided to have a look around the rest of the ground floor. Two adjoining large rooms stood apart from the rest of the house. In addition to being dark, they were crammed with armchairs and other furniture, decorated with carpets from Kasher and Esfahan, gleaming porcelain elephants from India, and Oriental chests with dragons embossed on five sides. The only wall that didn't contain reproductions of Chinese ideograms and watercolors of pagodas held a mirror that reproduced all the objects in the room, creating a chaotic display of stuff dusted and polished daily, as if these rooms were oblivious to permanence or even to human contact. Over the large windows hung red velvet drapes; only one tiny rectangle of light poked through where the drapes were out of place. A piece of paper in the corner near the windows caught my attention. It looked like a child's drawing and was taped to the wall about a meter from the floor. From a distance, the colorful square was lost among onyx-topped end tables and crystal vases from Bohemia. On closer examination, I saw that the two main blotches of color actually consisted of a thousand different streaks, like minuscule tributaries of water banded in two distinct shades; a slender figure composed of just a few strokes was paddling a boat that looked as much out of the water as in it. Its course was also uncertain, because nothing in the drawing defined the boat's movement, and the land or horizon seemed to be beyond the piece of paper.

I was intrigued by this drawing, which clashed so with the sumptuous decor; as I studied it, something flared in my memory, the kind of thing that sends you back to a journey, a leap across years, decades. I asked Anastácia's daughter who had made the drawing; not only didn't she know, but she claimed never even to have noticed the square of paper on the wall in the parlor she cleaned and dusted every morning. So then I asked how life was going in Manaus these days and whether the child was hers or a stepdaughter, but her response to my litany of questions was simply to grunt and then once again retreat into her ancestral silence. I wanted to know when our mother had gone away but didn't ask. I simply said I was going to see Emilie. Then she looked directly at me for the first time, calm and slow; and finally pronounced her longest utterances of the entire time I was in town.

"Bring her some of that honey from the country; it's her favorite," she said as she wound the clock on the wall.

"Do you think she's awake by now?" I asked.

"They say your grandmother hasn't slept in a long while. She dreams day and night; she dreams about you and your brother and the fish she's going to buy at the market first thing in the morning. She's probably back from her shopping and talking to the animals by now."

Emilie's conversations with the animals, her dreams, her trip to the market just as the sun begins to reveal all the many nuances of green and lights up the dark blade of the river . . . this woman's words contained part of my past life, an inferno of memories, a paralyzed world awaiting movement. Of course Emilie had told her about us. She knew that we were brother and sister and that Emilie had adopted us. Most likely she knew about Emilie's own four children: Hakim and Samara Délia, who had become our uncle and aunt, and the other unnamable two, Emilie's savage sons, who had the devil tattooed on their bodies and a pair of fiery tongues.

It was already almost seven o'clock by the time I left

the house. I removed my notebook, the tape recorder, and the letters you sent me from Spain from my knapsack and set them on a small onyx table beside the child's drawing in the parlor. I left my watch on, out of distraction or habit, never imagining I would consult it a thousand times that day, sometimes for no particular reason, sometimes to try to make time fly or at least take an unexpected leap. Outside, the light was still tenuous. Gazing at the stillness of the garden, Anastácia's daughter declared: "The rain's going to hold off."

That's when it happened. With incredible precision. I can't really say whether there was an interval between the chiming of the clock and the ringing of the telephone; the two sounds were simultaneous and seemed to belong to the same deep source. The coincidence of sounds lasted only seconds, and the moment the phone stopped ringing, the little girl hurled her doll's head at the weights of the clock, producing a sequence of ponderous and deranged chords, like a piano badly out of tune. The two weights were still clanging against each other when I heard the last toll of the church bell. Only then did I run to answer the phone, but when I picked it up there was only a buzz.

Before leaving to see Emilie, I thought of you in Barcelona, between La Sagrada Familia and the Mediterranean Sea, sitting on a bench in the Plaza del Diamante perhaps, maybe even thinking of me, of my journey back to our childhood: an imaginary city founded one morning in 1954. . . .

You were still crawling that Christmas and Soraya Ângela was my playmate. You often whimpered when she appeared, eager to play with you and fondle you; her wild eyes and abrupt gestures were enough to scare anyone. None of the neighborhood children would play with her, and she knew this, resigning herself to friendly mischief with the animals, climbing astride the sheep, pulling their ears, tying knots in the monkeys' tails. She carried on with a fury that was truly frightening, but afterward she would laugh and gaze at us calmly with those great dark eyes, as if to announce that some marvelous sign were imminent: perhaps a single word, we hoped, even badly articulated, or a syllable blurted out in impatience or rebellion? No such portent or small miracle was ever forthcoming, but that

Christmas Eve in 1954 Anastácia Socorro burst into the kitchen yelling, "She knows how to write!" and everyone ran out to the garden: all three of Emilie's sons, her friends and neighbors, her brother Emílio and, at the head of the group, Samara Délia, who spent her waking hours attending novenas and scouring the papers for news of a medical breakthrough that might restore her daughter's two missing senses. Then Emilie rushed in, and everyone stepped back so that she could see Soraya Ângela squatting in the white lilies, a chunk of red chalk in her left hand, completing the last stroke of a very familiar name on Sálua the turtle's shell.

"It was the best Christmas present ever!" Emilie exclaimed later, after reading her name, scrawled letter by careful letter, across the turtle's back. Samara Délia was radiant. For the first time her brothers were looking at their niece as a human being rather than a monster.

Many years after Soraya Ângela's death, in a conversation before I left Manaus, Aunt Samara confided that she regretted her happiness in that moment.

"I was still so naïve," she said. "I thought my brothers had finally forgiven me for having her, but it was all an act to get sympathy from my mother; all the fuss and congratulations were for her benefit, and it worked. They fawned over Soraya just like they pretended respect for my father so he'd give them the house key and some pocket money to go paint the town. When I told Mother what they were up to, do you know what she said? She said, 'I don't believe it! Your daughter was born deaf and dumb and now you're becoming unfeeling? Your brothers adore you! They're insensitive at times but that's only because they're boys: adolescence is a time for rebellion.' "

"They were adolescents, all right, and they were shameless," continued Aunt Samara. "When Sorainha died they had the audacity to order Swiss organdy flowers from Madame Verdade. I think they must have anticipated her death because right after the accident all these fabric flowers appeared out of nowhere. I never felt so humiliated. Six years without a word to me, without even acknowledging her existence, and the minute she's dead they spend a fortune to cover her with flowers!"

I don't know if you remember Soraya Ângela, her sorry life and her horrible death. She used to crawl along after you, wanting to play, and the two of you loved to go around and collect all the sapodilla fruit that had teeth marks from bats. You were always so frightened if you woke up to find a little black cluster of bats hanging from the ceiling in your room, and the next day I'd show you the hole in the screen where they came in, content until the day's brightness sent them out to the dark cave in the crown of the jambo tree to suck nectar from the fruit.

You weren't home that morning. Emilie had taken you to the market, the uncles were sleeping, and Samara Délia had been at the store with Grandpa since dawn. It all happened so fast and so unexpectedly, as if some cruel stroke of fate were out to get poor Soraya. The two of us were alone in the front yard looking for fruit the bats had nibbled. Well, I was the one actually gathering the fruit, still wet with dew, and also picking poppies, plucking blossoms off the jambo tree, and throwing them all in a basket. Whenever Soraya joined in collecting fruits and flowers, she did so in her own curious way, sitting for a long time staring at the flesh of the velvet heart that is the jambo fruit, or slowly breathing in the fragrance of the poppies and orchids and other flowers. Later I realized she was trying to use smell and sight to compensate for her lack of speech and hearing. Other times, as on that morning, Soraya contented herself by playing with the rag doll Emilie had made her. I remember the doll's face perfectly. It had jutting black eyes, the cheeks of an angel, and if you looked closely you could see that only the ears and mouth were flat, stitched with red thread, a special artifice of Emilie's. Soraya never let the doll out of her sight; she made poppy garlands for it, offered it pieces of fruit, clutched it in her arms when she clambered astride the sheep, and took it to bed with her in a tight embrace. These were glorious days, days full of discoveries. Eventually Soraya began to look like a frightened somnambulist, seeming more and more withdrawn; she drew strange, generally serpentine shapes on the tablecloth, on the walls, on the uneven mosaic tile surrounding the fountain, and on Sálua's shell, where Emilie's name was still visible. On one of the few occasions Aunt Samara actually talked about her daughter, she reported catching Soraya one night in front of the Venetian mirror in the bedroom, applying makeup to her doll's lips and cheeks; one little face looking at the other, and the mirror separating them farther from the world.

"Seeing her like that, so enthralled . . . I actually tiptoed away so as not to disturb her. It was the first and only time in five years that I completely forgot Soraya was deaf!"

I've never been able to understand Samara Délia's silence, the way she seemed not to want even to know how it happened. There I was, dumbstruck, staring out at the street, and that muffled thud that seemed to float in the steam rising from the gray paving stones. I looked for Soraya everywhere, behind tree trunks and bushes, pretending I'd find her, clinging absurdly to the idea that she had run out back to see the animals, to take a bath in the fountain, to hop the fence into the chicken coop and wave her arms furiously at the chickens so they'd stir from sleep to chaotic flight, unfurling their wings, scratching at earth and air, fluttering wildly, trapped between the unsurmountable fence and the frail figure who didn't threaten them in the least with her excessive contortions. Scenes like this inspired amazement and commiseration in all of us who witnessed them from time to time, but for Soraya it was like a party, a way for a child without access to words to be heard and noticed, it was a parenthesis in the everyday life of chicken coop, yard, animals, providing an escape from the stares and whispers: she can't talk, can't hear, her body's just a flurry of gestures, the centerpiece of a public spectacle seen through complacent eyes. Emilie herself would serve you and Soraya at mealtimes, peeling fruit and ladling portions of food onto your plates, her hands in constant motion; but you already had words enough—monosyllables at least—to accept or reject what was offered, while Soraya could only push the plate away, shake her head, or tilt it toward someone in silent supplication. Sometimes she'd look at you, at your babyish mouth, perhaps thinking: When did I lose words? or At what moment did I discover that I couldn't talk?—perhaps annoyed that you, at your young age, could already construct sentences—unfinished, disconnected sentences, it's true, but with a movement of your lips, someone would react, someone would move their lips, and the world around you existed.

People came running from the street, from the barracks nearby, from the neighboring houses, and then Emilie appeared among them, holding your hand, her eyes searching for mine. I had stayed in my hiding place in the crest of the jambo tree, until finally deciding to dash blindly upstairs for help. Upstairs everything seemed serene and alien to what was going on outside. I ran down the hall to the bedrooms and lurched to a stop in front of Uncle Hakim, asleep in the hammock. I listened to his rhythmic breathing, eager yet afraid to wake him. In the half-light I could just make out the enormous pile of books he read over and over again. Do you remember how you used to perch on top of the pile while Uncle Hakim thumbed through one of the books to find an engraving that illustrated an impending crime, a love scene, or the death of a protagonist? You'd sound out each complicated name in a guttural stammer, and after listening to your rendition of some Slavic name, Hakim would make fun of everyone, including himself, claiming the correct pronunciation could only come from the mouth of a two-year-old child, or from Soraya. Of the three uncles, Hakim was the only one who'd kid around with us. He'd stroll hand in hand with Soraya, on the sly of course, for fear that Aunt Samara would find out and throw in his face the phrase she'd been repeating ever since Soraya was born: "None of you is worthy to so much as touch my daughter." But Hakim wasn't intimidated by his sister's warning, though he knew she had her reasons to prohibit any contact between Soraya and the uncles. And Samara Délia clearly had her suspicions about the strolls those two had begun taking in the months before Christmas 1954. At lunch, with everyone there, Aunt Samara and Uncle Hakim would share their embarrassment wordlessly when confronted with Soraya's antics imitating a sloth climbing a tree; her body frozen into the immobility of the bronze sentinels planted in front of the barracks; her wild gesticulations evoking the Sicilian twins conversing with a dog. Nothing escaped her attention, as if to prove that seeing was sufficient in itself to interpret or reproduce the world. Little by little we grew accustomed to Soraya's renditions of the daily sights on the city's streets, the way her flailing arms and legs captured a diversity of incidents and bizarre characters, like the twins who told an endless story to their dog at exactly the same time every morning on the same park bench under an acacia tree. Soraya imitated all three, a flurry of lightning gestures alternating with a sudden expression of interest and incomprehension, eyes wide, crouched on all fours. Then she'd suddenly clap her hands out in front of her, elbows locked open, while tilting and swaying wildly. With the exception of the other two uncles, everybody would laugh uproariously at these antics, which went on all through lunch until nap time. Caught somewhere between laughter and perplexity, I wondered why, after each chortle, Emilie's face would close into a frown. A sign she disapproved of those morning jaunts, I suppose. Aunt Samara feigned indifference, but deep down she was worried about all the showing off, though she didn't put a stop to Soraya's sporadic outings with Uncle Hakim. It would have been worse to watch her daughter grow up confined to the house alone, with nothing to do but pick fruits and flowers and get stung digging up anthills.

"I thanked God every time I saw Soraya clutching her doll, running around having fun like any other little girl. But after the accident there wasn't a doll in the world I could stand to look at," she told me the day I went to visit her to tell her about my trip.

She was still living and working at the Parisian then, and she had such a knack for the business that Grandfather permanently assigned her the delicate and dreaded job even he preferred to avoid: attempting to fathom the customers' tastes and selecting and ordering the merchandise. Samara rarely came to the house, and beyond her activities at the Parisian, her life was a mystery to all of us. Grandfather remarked vaguely that she traveled a couple of times a year, though no one knew the destination or reason for these trips. Her absence was so brief and unexpected that Grandfather would just announce at lunch: "Samara's back."

One day, after he pronounced this toneless phrase, one of his sons added, "Back from her secret home away from home . . ."

By this time Grandfather no longer had the stomach for fury and debate, much less harsh reprimands of the two sons he used to call brutes, threatening them with the belt. After Soraya Ângela was born, he had simply tried to tone them down occasionally, but when various attempts came to nothing he resigned himself to declaring he was no longer concerned with the fate of his sons. As a patriarch of advanced age and fatigue, he spent hours playing backgammon and telling you stories, and he fervently and extravagantly praised his daughter in all she did, to the point that Emilie was totally bewildered.

"I give up," she'd stammer. "I have no idea where his illusions end and his lucidity begins."

Actually, Grandfather proved himself more lucid than ever in praising his daughter. His fame as a hardheaded, stern, and maniacal man had become diluted with time, but one unanimous truth emerged from all the ready analysis of his character: he was above all a generous person who cultivated solitude. It was Grandfather who helped me break away from Manaus and go away to study, and, since the day Emilie snuggled us into her lap until the moment of separation, he had never opposed our presence in the house. We enjoyed the same pleasures and privileges as their natural children, and endured the same storms of anger and bad humor of a despondent father and a heartsick mother. Nothing and no one excluded us from the family, but at the appropriate moment Grandfather made it his business to explain to us who we were and where we came from, in as few words as possible, with no hint of pity or excess of drama.

During my short visit with Aunt Samara, she often lamented Hakim's absence. "It's been almost ten years since he left and he's never written me a line," she said with a stab of resentment. Other than this, the events of the past no longer seemed to torment her as they used to, which is probably why she could speak of them easily, with no sign of rancor. But while Aunt Samara's face wore an affable expression, she still clothed her body in mourning: black knit dress, black lace hairnet molding her black hair, and a string of black pearls that had belonged to Emilie. And she had the same reserved and standoffish way about her; she still insisted on posing in profile and looking at you sideways as she talked. More often than not, she returned to memories of her daughter:

"Such a pretty little imp, with curly light hair and the body of a gazelle. I wake up in the morning anxious to look at her picture, like someone hurrying to pluck a rose. Emilie? Yes, she visits the Parisian occasionally and comes into my room to cry. I never know who she's crying for or what makes her saddest. Hakim's absence? The death of her brother, or of Soraya? Her two wild sons?"

She peered at me, her face still turned to the side.

"I never needed any of them, you know, but Emilie . . . How could I live without her?"

No one could live without Emilie, no more than we could deny her her many eccentricities. Emilie insisted, for example, on saving Soraya's doll, which had survived the accident unharmed, and stashing it away with her own things, instead of allowing it to be burned as Aunt Samara requested. Uncle Hakim had snatched the doll from the children right after the accident. When I woke him up in his hammock, his glasses, which he'd pushed up onto his forehead, crashed to the floor. He seemed to have a hard time waking. I think he was still savoring the images of some wonderful dream, because at first he just smiled at me and sighed, "Beautiful," and closed his eyes again; so I shook the hammock, hard, threw my precious flowers and fruit seeds in his face, and stammered I don't even know what, pointing to the street: the site of the disaster. He opened his eyes and leapt up, and as I dove for the hammock I kept thinking about the flash of light in the middle of the street, and worrying about you, searching for you, but all I'd seen was Emilie stooped over a shape under a red-stained sheet. Fish and vegetables and fruit lay scattered about on the paving stones, and soldiers swung clubs at the kids who tried to make off with the contents of Emilie's basket, which lay perilously close to Soraya's body; a couple of the more daring street kids jumped back and forth over the bloodstain, taunting the men in their khaki twill, the same shade as the children's skin.

In the intense sunlight everyone seemed to be made of bronze; the only discordant notes were the flowers blooming on Emilie's skirt and the red stain still spreading along the sheet that had become a cocoon, the head like a hat, or the most intense, most concentrated red, as if the color had exploded there, at the extremity. It was one of the most painful images of my childhood; maybe that's why I've mentioned it in several of my letters. You wrote that I was privileged, lucky, because all this took place when I could already, for better or worse, fix it in memory. In one of your letters you said: "Life truly begins with memory, and you remember perfectly the four gold bracelets on Emilie's wrist that fateful, sunny morning, the flowers embroidered on her dress. What a privilege to be able to remember all that. Me, in my sailor suit—I had no part in the general panic and sadness, I remember simply that Soraya existed and that she was taller than me; I vaguely remember her hands touching my face and how much she liked animals. Her disappearance, if it didn't pass unnoticed, was an enigma to me; as Emilie would tell me over the following years: 'Your cousin went on a trip. . . .' I learned, from you, that I had practically witnessed her death. Some witness. Where was I that morning?"

You spent the day talking about the fish and animals you'd seen at the market, incapable of understanding the turmoil and despair that had overtaken the house. You were wearing one of the little linen nightshirts on which Emilie had embroidered two horses' heads or, rather, the outlines of heads and manes, so that the transparency of the fabric let your skin fill in the color. Beneath the nightshirt you wore a pair of soldier's boots and white knee socks with your initials embroidered on them in Gothic letters. You were a bundle of incongruity from head to toe: boots, embroidery, high socks, Emilie's extravagances all. She'd set you up in a high chair, your feet dangling, and you'd get vertigo looking down at the floor as if it were an abyss and you propped above it, immobile: a statue or toy for the adults who admired you, pinched your cheeks, examined your profile, any small part of your body that was visible as you sat on your throne under the trellis on the smaller patio, protected from the sun by a roof of plants. It kind of bothered me to see you that way, surrounded by women with powdered faces, smiling masks by the light of day, wanting to devour you; your tiniest gesture provoked an uproar, a convulsion, with all of them snatching up their fans and fighting for a place beside you, desperate to stir the air around Emilie's little idol.

Emilie took great delight in these sessions of idolatry; she enjoyed her position as the great mother, hovering over you like a radiant, perpetually inflatable bell jar, and I must confess that it was almost humiliating for the other children to witness one of these scenes of devotion and ecstasy; after all, who wouldn't have liked to be up there, a newborn saint wafting on the breezes of adulation and colorful, madly waving fans. You floated, unsuspecting, in a niche of spikenard. Later, once you turned two, the pedestal was abolished, and you were allowed to find your place on the ground and walk alone, but still you were surrounded by a wall of women exuding odors as strange as their names: Mentaha, Hindié, Yasmine. You missed Soraya Ângela traipsing around after you, your two heads bent over the dirt searching for fire ants, following the seemingly endless trail, randomly choosing one sinuous line that vanished at the foot of a tree; there you would stop and follow the line back in the other direction to the flower bed at the back of the garden beside the patio with the fountain; finally, you'd find the little hills with holes on top and lines of ants coming and going: subterranean homes, invisible labyrinths, movable mounds, growing, disappearing here, reappearing there. You already knew these anthills and their holes like eyes in the earth burned like fire, but Soraya amused herself poking at them. Once she rubbed her face against a small mound, then got up and ran like a shot to the fountain; her cheek looked as if it were completely on fire, and all the agony of her inexistent voice was fixed in her facial contortions, her eyes squeezed shut, her hands thrashing at the edge of the enormous stone seashell, looking for something, liquid to alleviate her pain, the streams of water from the mouths of stone angels; then you no-

ticed Soraya was gone and, abandoned among castles
and caves of fire, unprotected by the shadow of her
body, you cried and cried, you cried buckets, even after
looking up toward the fountain and seeing her swollen
face, a smile emerging beneath beads of water and clusters of ringlets. It was like an inversion of torture and
pain—one crying for an absence, the other smiling to
discover the reason for the crying. You quieted down
when she returned from the fountain, her cupped
hands sprinkling you with water, luring you off to the
mosaics on the patio, to the fountain, to the brown,
convex rock pretending to sleep its century-old sleep,
that strange sculpture that sometimes awakened near
the fountain, invisible on the rough stonework—so invisible that it was useless, later, even to look for it. How
many times did I scour the yard, the side hallway, and
both patios to no avail? It was frustrating not to be able
to find the hiding place of such a slow, hundred-year-
old beast but, after all, slowness, which we see as a defi-
ance or an affront, is what it's made of. I'd find it by
accident, more often than not, camouflaged under a
heap of leaves on the ground. It would simply reveal itself, usually more by movement than by contrast of tex-
tures, as opposed to animals that lack its bony shell,
which looks as if it's meant to be exposed to time,
weather, the world. Peeking through the wooden slats
of the shutters, I'd watch you and Soraya playing beside the black clock, that grotto with golden weights,
which had for decades matched Emilie day for day in
the repetitive cycle of passing time; that clock on the

wall, the most silent I've ever seen, was one of the things that fascinated Soraya the most. She'd sit in front of it for hours, her eye following the pendulum, the minute hand, waiting for the silent jump of the black arrow. I keep thinking how much of her life she dedicated to this voiceless dialogue with time, indifferent to the din when the two arrows met; suffice it to say that at noon the deep and violent clanging hurt my ears, and I'd run as far away from the sonorous source as possible. No one could tolerate that noise, the way it suddenly fell down around you like thunder. I remember from a very young age watching Soraya sit, impassive, before that big black thing, just as it was about to announce midday; at first I thought it was a trick, but she didn't even shift her gaze when Emilie approached the clock each day at noon. Immersed in an atmosphere of pure reverberation, Emilie would open the glass door, reach for something in a corner of the case, and grope around the interior walls until her hand emerged with a key and then disappeared in the metal innards searching for the hole, the slot the key would fit, there in the heart of the machine.

The big black clock was the only thing in the whole house that Soraya Ângela worshiped. Uncle Hakim, who was full of strange stories about the clock, told me it only came to live on the wall in the parlor after months of delicate negotiation between Emilie and the man from Marseilles who sold the Parisian to the family in the thirties. The transaction threatened to fall through more than once due to their mutual intransigence, until Grandfather finally threw in Emilie's face the possibility that the whole deal might go down the drain because of a clock.

"If you keep this up, we'll be on a boat back to Lebanon empty-handed," he warned her.

"Fine!" replied Emilie. "That's where the clock I really want is. And, besides, then I wouldn't have to stammer or lay my hands on a dictionary just to say what's on my mind."

After four months of proposals and counterproposals, it was finally agreed that not just the clock but also the Venetian mirrors and lamps, the art deco chairs, and a set of silver cutlery with ivory handles would be Emilie's; for her part in the patient and obstinate game of back-and-forth, she would give the Frenchman two pieces of imported fabric from Lyons and a parrot with a strong Midi accent who could say "Marseilles," "La France," and "Soyez le bien venu." It was very painful for Emilie to part with the parrot, because she'd been a gift from Hindié Conceição, who had invested many hours instructing it in the art of speaking well. From her hanging domicile set up in the middle of the patio out back of the Parisian, Laure would call out the Ave Maria, recite a verse from Deuteronomy, and at twilight or sunny mornings she'd sing the two women's favorite song, "Baladi Baladi," with Emilie clapping along in time. At nightfall the most inattentive customers and visitors would think they were listening to some short-wave radio transmission of a novena or mass taking place on the other side of the globe. Grandfather was apparently famous for announcing that "here in Amazonas, those who parrot the words of the apostles wear colorful feathers and crap on the heads of the infidels." Emilie knew that Laure's giving forth hymns in the voice of a wind-up toy irritated her husband to the point of making him steer clear of the patio. But she only began to become disenchanted with the bird after Laure took a dislike to one of the maids who worked for the family before Anastácia Socorro came on the scene. Emilie had chosen this black orphan girl from among the many abandoned children at the Brazilian Assistance Legion; she was so hungry and sad that she'd forgotten both her first and last names and communicated only through gestures and sighs. Laure disliked the newcomer from the first: she refused the bananas and papaya and tapioca with milk the girl brought her, and stopped singing or praying whenever she came onto the patio. Emilie tolerated this obstinacy for a while but finally fired the girl the day Laure awoke to find her beak glued shut with a mixture of thick spittle and salt. The bird had been silent ever since. During the months of negotiation with the man from Marseilles, Hindié had taken the parrot home with her and worked with her feverishly. Not only was she able to get Laure talking again, but she even managed to teach her some phrases in French. The man was so impressed with the bird's phonetic agility that he built her a new home, a huge bamboo cage, and, in spite of the bird's sex, rebaptized her Strabon. The patrons and French visitors to the Ville de Paris restaurant on rua do Sol were amazed to find an enormous cage suspended from the ceiling fan, swaying and spinning like a gigantic mobile halfway between the ceiling and the floor. It was only after the blades of the fan stopped turning that Strabon became visible, cowering on her perch, feathers ruffled, head tucked under her wing. Without the gusts of wind, the bird became herself again: her iridescent plumage and haughty manner on display, she'd cry out the newest addition to her repertoire: "Je vais à Marseille, pas toi?" A few laughed without understanding; many grew sad because Strabon's intended destination was closed to them and its mention only heightened their longing for distant Midi. Emilie was furious when she heard about the Frenchman's harebrained idea that exposing Laure to the fan's artificial windstorm would help her acclimatize more readily to the cold wind of the European winter. She finally decided to go to the restaurant and speak her mind, but stopped short at the door when she saw the entire French community of Manaus, shoulder to shoulder and surrounded by bottles of wine and champagne, craning their necks to gaze worshipfully at the parrot in the cage above their heads, who, accompanied by a blind man on the accordion, was leading them in a booming rendition of the "Marseillaise."

Emilie returned home exasperated. "With all the strutting roosters around here, they choose a parrot as the symbol of the Fatherland! Next thing you know they'll be painting my poor Laure red, white, and blue."

Emilie's apparent obsession to acquire the clock remained a mystery to Grandfather—to all of us—for a long time. If there was anything analagous between Tripoli and Manaus, it certainly wasn't the port life of Manaus, with its profusion of open-air markets, peddlers and fishmongers hawking their wares to crowds of dark-skinned people. It was, really, the differences, more than the similarities, that first struck those who disembarked here, precisely because a change of ports almost always presupposes a change of life: oceanscape, snow-covered mountains, salt sea, unfamiliar religious architecture, and, above all, God's name spoken in another tongue. But one analogy prevailed: in Manaus as in Tripoli, it was not a clock that heralded the day's first activity nor determined its last: sunlight, birdsong, human noise, these penetrated the sanctuary most remote from the street, these inaugurated the day; and silence proclaimed the night. Emilie followed the course of the sun, indifferent to clock time, to the tolling of the bells at Nossa Senhora dos Remédios and to the bugle call that floated over from the barracks three times a day. She detested the very idea of someone blowing a horn at six-hour intervals, the sound spreading over the roofs of a city whose inhabitants could perfectly well wake to the sound of roosters. With or without buglers, the sunny morning would break, unexpected, impetuous, in the middle of a crow. Which is why Grandfather found it so odd that Emilie was so intent on getting that clock. And then she made a point of bringing it to the new house as soon as it was finished; the mirrors and other furniture were installed later, after the Parisian became merely a place of business.

I, too, was always very eager to figure out why Emilie was so interested in the clock. I knew that of all the uncles, only Hakim was a potential source of secrets. By the time his plane landed, Emilie had already died. He arrived early Friday evening, after a ten-hour flight with many stopovers. His suitcases contained an exorbitant quantity of Eastern delicacies and a box of indispensable Persian tobacco to feed the vice of the oldest Levantines, who smoked only native Tehran tobacco in their water pipes. Hakim was somewhat hopeful when he arrived, because Uncle Emílio, ever discreet and cautious, hadn't told his nephew the whole story. He had said only that Emilie was more sad and homesick than aged, and urged him to come before sunset on Friday. Uncle Hakim agreed without insisting on talking to Emilie, knowing that his mother was half deaf and could only understand two or three people's voices besides Hindié Conceição, so that talking to her meant bellowing loudly and slowly, and in Arabic. When we returned from the cemetery early that evening, we found Hakim alone in the deserted backyard. Impatient that he couldn't go inside, he was looking through the window grates at the parlor plunged in chaos, feeling a sinister foreboding that he realized was justified when he saw the approaching line of cars and the dark clothes of the women who came to greet him. He seemed confused, the way he ran his hands through his graying hair, hurrying to regain his composure and adjust his linen jacket, because the welcome that would have been effusive and warm after so much time away amounted to no more than a handshake or a hug of condolence. People gathered in a circle around him. Some sat down on his suitcases to cry, and others wandered in their minds through the untidy parlor lit by a single lamp, searching for the vestiges of a whole lifetime, postponing the difficult decision to enter the parlor that still smelled of fresh flowers and candle wax. Finally Uncle Hakim was able to speak. He, too, had been overcome by sudden pain, and I stood and listened to his halting voice, which asked and answered at the same time, a voice with no other concern but to stay aloft so that Emilie's brother and friends would have a reprieve from grieving over the disaster that had taken place at daybreak. Uncle Emílio took advantage of a pause to announce my presence and beckoned to me with such vehemence that he seemed to be denouncing my strange manner, my role as passive observer. For a moment mourning gave way to effusion; Uncle Hakim and I embraced, and the whole time he held me in his arms he was cursing, bemoaning how we'd lived so long in the south in neighboring states and I'd only come to visit him once in God knows how long. The weight of age on his body had made him slightly hunchbacked, but he was still as elegant as ever and had acquired the noncommittal gallantry of a lonely and good-natured bachelor. He asked someone to open the door, since he wanted to hand out the presents and sit awhile in the armchair he recognized from bygone days. Hindié, who knew the house like the back of her hand, turned on the lights and disappeared, insisting she was going to make coffee. Uncle Hakim decided to open his suitcases immediately, to hide his uneasy sense that everything and everyone was still under Emilie's dense shadow. He distributed colorful packages all around, even to those he didn't know, and set the rest on the Persian rug for the friends he would see later. Just one package remained untouched, and soon enough I understood that it would never be opened. People smiled and thanked him for their gifts, all of which seemed to be perfect for the taste or size of the recipient; even so, there was not a great deal of enthusiasm. And as Uncle Hakim asked a bit about each person's life, a halo of death hovered over each reticent answer. There was nothing to do but surrender, without fear or regret, to the pain he had been trying so hard to hide. And so Hakim began sharing his loss and his memories, but in such an exaggerated, almost fierce way that Hindié Conceição was soon trembling from head to toe and almost collapsed with her tray full of coffee. I myself was so taken aback that I didn't notice the arrival of some friends of Emilie's, who had seen the house lit up and the doors open and been drawn inside by the voice of a son magnetizing the others' attention with reminiscences of his mother:

"Remember Emilie and her coffee grounds?" asked Uncle Hakim, taking a last sip of his coffee. "She'd ask everyone to set their cups on the tray and then she'd study the bottom of each, reading the tangled black lines of dried coffee and grounds to tell the fate of each person."

The conversation went on into the night, because no one could listen to all the stories without adding an opinion or memory of his or her own; someone had already begun opening boxes of candies and sweets to accompany the next round of coffee. After that would come juices and brandies and, who knows, maybe even an improvised meal in the wee hours. All this had me thinking how eager I was to learn more about Emilie's life before we came to live with her. I took advantage of the loud and weepy testimonials to tiptoe out of the parlor, intending to leave without a word to anyone. But before I got out the door, Uncle Hakim came hurrying after me to say goodbye.

"Is there any news from Samara Délia?" he asked.

"No," I told him. "All I know is what Uncle Emílio told me: that she left the Parisian and that no one has any idea where she is."

I asked how long he'd be staying in Manaus.

With a troubled air, looking around nervously as if expecting an intruder, he said:

"As long as it takes to find my sister."

I told Uncle Hakim that I wanted to talk to him away from all the chaos, away from everyone. I mentioned the black clock, and some of the other things that had me intrigued; he promised to meet with me as soon as he'd had a chance to catch his breath.

"I could spend the rest of my life talking about the past," he said, in a much more untroubled voice.

Sunday night we sat down together beneath the trellis on the small patio, right under the windows to our old bedrooms. When Monday morning dawned Uncle Hakim was still talking, and he paused only to visit the animals and take a short stroll around the patio with the fountain, where he splashed water on his face and hair; then he returned, energized, his head swimming with scenes and conversations, as if he had just discovered the key to memory.

HAKIM

I WONDERED THE SAME thing when I was a teen-
ager, even before—for as long as I can remember. I
questioned Mama about the clock several times and,
after lots of evasions, she asked me if I remembered
what I used to say when I was little whenever I looked
at the full moon. I must have been around three when
I first pointed up at the sky and said "Look! The night
has a light in it!" That was her oblique explanation, her
way to avoid talking about herself.

It was only years later, after managing to pull some
information out of Hindié Conceição, that I began to
make some sense out of things. She told me about how
Mama and her two brothers, Emílio and Emir, were left

in Tripoli with relatives while Fadel and Samir, my grandparents, went to try their luck in a new land that would become Amazonas. Emilie couldn't bear the idea of such a long separation from her parents.

The morning they left, in Beirut, she ran off to the convent in Ebrin, which she'd heard about from her mother. Her two brothers scoured Mount Lebanon looking for her until, some two weeks later, a rumor began circulating that Fadel's daughter had become a novice at Ebrin. When Emir found out the rumor was true he made quite a scene, bursting into the convent without the slightest reverence for its pious and tranquil atmosphere, bellowing Emilie's name and demanding that she come to Mother Superior's office at once. Finally she appeared in the doorway, dressed all in white, her face framed by an organdy wimple. This vision, perhaps more than the fact of her running away, provoked him to put a gun to his head and insist he would pull the trigger unless she agreed to leave the convent. Emilie knelt at his feet and Mother Superior interceded, saying she should leave with her brother, for God would receive her anywhere in the world if it were her vocation to serve the Lord.

It was a terrible episode in Emilie's life. She agreed to leave the convent but begged to be allowed to spend the rest of the morning praying and to ring the bell in the passage beside the cloister twelve times at midday to announce the end of prayers. Emilie had been assigned this job because of her fascination with a black clock that darkened one of the white walls of the Vice-

Superior's office. The first time Emilie walked into the room, precisely at noon, she had stood agape, ecstatic to hear the sound of the twelve chimes, before Sister Virginie Boulad had even uttered a word. Hindié Conceição said many times that Emilie always closed her eyes whenever she mentioned that crystalline moment.

Her voice would sound grave and melodious and seemed to come from somewhere between heaven and earth the way it expanded in the air like the warm grace of God emanating from the Eternal and His Word. And she compared the succession of chimes to the thousand secret voices of the bell that calms agonized nights and wakes the faithful to come to the altar where repentance, innocence, and adversity are evoked through silence and meditation. Perhaps that's why Emilie's life stopped each time the almost imperceptible echo of the Remédios church bell soared up and broke like a cloud above the patio where she was polishing the stone angels after scrubbing off the mold and slime accumulated over a season of torrential rains. She'd stop what she was doing, forget whatever instructions she was calling to Anastácia, and sit contemplating the sky, as if high in the clouds unfurling against brilliant blue she expected to see the elongated black box with its glass door, its golden numerals, pointing hands, and shiny pendulum.

That's all Hindié told me about the clock and about my mother's stay in the convent of Ebrin more than half a century ago. She rattled on and on, the stem of the water pipe in one hand and a remarkable fan made of painted and braided bird feathers in the other, pausing only long enough to catch her breath or wipe the sweat from her face with a corner of her skirt, unconcerned about displaying the layers of transparent fabric between her skin and her ubiquitous flowered cotton shift. Besides appearing utterly natural to Hindié, this seemingly shameless gesture created an almost familial intimacy between her and the "children" of the house. (Though I was almost eighteen years old, my frail body and timid nature accentuated the age difference between us.) As Hindié fanned herself with a wrist movement that involved her whole body, I felt the intermittent stream of tepid air and smoke in my face and followed her voice without interrupting, not that there would have been much of a chance of breaking in on the sinuous thread of that one-way conversation. Hindié possessed such a great will to talk that in a split second of monologue she was capable of moving seamlessly from yesterday's bad mood to one Christmas Eve long ago when we were still living at the Parisian.

On Christmas Eve everyone gathered in the kitchen to help with the preparations, except Father, who would shut himself up in his room or go to spend the day at Floating City—built on huge tree trunks in the water near the port—stepping in and out of the huts to chat with friends and newly arrived river people from the interior, after which he'd walk to the port to visit the shops and boats.

Emilie would get me up before dawn to gather flowers from the garden; then we'd drag Samara out of the hammock and take the trolley to the French district to buy bouquets of crepe jasmine and pink bougainvillea. Once home, we set to work with wooden needles and yellow thread making necklaces and garlands for the guests, while Emilie placed one white petal in each porcelain cup and scattered the orange-leafed jasmine here and there on the floor. The neighborhood women helped in the kitchen, mixing and rolling out the dough for the hors d'oeuvre pastries and baklava. Paper-fine sheets of dough were hung all over the house, transluscent curtains forming tenuous patches of shade where we'd play at trying to guess each other's silhouettes or draping it over our faces like a mask or a hood. Uncle Emílio always did the shopping and butchered the sheep; he would also wring the necks of the chickens and cut their throats with a knife so the blood could run freely, as my father required. Only one other butchering method was ever used: one Christmas the birds were fed cane liquor until they were falling-down drunk, at which point their necks were twisted until their already blurred world spun like a top. They died slowly, their eyes live coals and their necks ragged as twine. "Suffering like that can only be the work of a Christian," pronounced my father, well aware that Hindié used this method at other people's houses and that it was a common enough practice in the city.

Hindié had shown up that Christmas Eve with a big jug of *cachaça* and proceeded to get twelve chickens and four turkeys stone drunk. Then she wound a strong thread of palm around their necks and invited the neighbors to witness the carnage. I have never been able to shake the image of those wobbly-necked birds hopping around in circles, strangling themselves, and each other, with each leap. Hindié clapped and guffawed, shamelessly showing her toothless gums and completely indifferent to the clouds of flies clinging to the thatch of hair that fell to the middle of her back.

I remember observing everything from a distance that afternoon, full of curiosity and a certain apprehension. Hindié treated all children as if they were her own, providing a ready stream of kisses, hugs, and teasing words to all the small victims who lived near her. But this outpouring of affection sometimes seemed the manifestation of a consummate sadism, since her exaggerated attentions made us physically uncomfortable and lacked the transcendence and naturalness of true maternal gestures, which are warm and sensual without excess or ostentation. Maybe that's why I felt smothered and besieged in Hindié's presence—not so much because she was ugly and unkempt but because of the way she pursued or, better, persecuted me, her arms flung wide and flapping with excitement, so that from a child's-eye view they looked like enormous and threatening tentacles. Hindié always announced her arrival with much tumultuous clapping, shouting "Emilie" in that toothless voice of hers that echoed through all the rooms of the Parisian.

Samara and I would scurry off to hide in the far corners of the house, where we remained cocooned in a hammock, rocking to the vibrations from the booming voice that prowled the house in search of us. But the most repulsive thing about Hindié was her smell, a sourness that hovered about her like a halo of fetid perfume. Childhood is full of unforgettable smells. During my years away from Manaus, I don't know if I would have been able to visualize Hindié, but how could I forget the warm air she exuded, which bullied me like the gush of an eternal wind even at a distance? My father said Hindié smelled nastier than a polecat. "If that woman walked into the jungle," he'd whisper with a twinkle, "every jaguatirica in heat would come lick her legs."

The fact is, ever since that Christmas, my father and Hindié have gone out of their way to avoid each other. To this day I'm not sure how he discovered that the chickens and turkeys had been given liquor before they were strangled. Hindié, who was as hard on my father as he was on her, pronounced that Father's nose was keener than a dog's.

"He picked up the scent of cachaça out there in the yard, where the smell of white jasmine is overpowering!"

As soon as Father appeared, looking arrogant but judicious, and without a greeting for anyone, we had the sinking feeling that an evening traditionally given over to merriment and gluttony now hung by a taut and fragile thread, which might well be broken at the zenith of laughter, flirtation, dancing, and loud praise for the culinary exhuberance and the kaleidoscopic decoration of the parlor.

In one corner stood the pine tree pretending to be a cedar, heavy with ornaments and surrounded by colorful presents wrapped in silk paper; the shelves of the showcases and china closets were lined with trays of sweets, all kinds of bonbons, dried fruits, and various local fruit pies. The parlor ceiling was hung with iridescent balloons, and the house was littered with kapok-tree balls rolled in crepe paper, each containing a tiny box of caramels and chocolate-covered nuts. There was so much color, so many sparkling and glittery things everywhere, that the party was reminiscent of pre-carnival festivities; the lack of masks and costumes seemed to be the only thing keeping this religious repast from turning into a pagan festival.

Loud hand-clapping accompanied Portuguese and Middle-Eastern music on the Victrola as neighbors from other countries, dressed for the occasion, came to greet Emilie and to watch Mentaha's daughters dance. The evening would have ended in disaster, though, if not for Emilie and one unexpected visitor.

My father had confined himself to his room from dusk on, straight through most of the evening; we all felt that his refusal to join the party transcended discretion and represented a silent revolt. And while Emilie seemed utterly absorbed in the activity around her, she was not unaware that people around her were worried, sensing an imminent storm.

"I told your mother she should go talk to him, but you know Emilie, she's not one for wheedling," said Hindié. "And I asked her why he was so upset."

"Some infraction of one of the commandments from the Book, no doubt," cracked Emilie. "But today I'm going to be the one who says what can and can't be done, not some illiterate soldier who calls himself Prophet and Enlightened One."

The houseful of revelers heard footsteps and then the dry crack of a door slamming shut. Everyone fell silent, but a thoughtful hand turned up the volume on the Victrola. Even so, no one but Emilie managed to look natural or spontaneous; everyone stood frozen, as if in a stiff family portrait. Father stalked through the two parlors and the shop area, just as haughty as before, and nodded blindly to people without registering who they were. Those who considered extending their hands were relieved to see his arms loaded with enough provisions for a trek across the desert: a water pipe inlaid with mother-of-pearl, a water jug full of dried pumpkin seeds, a package of bread and zaartar, and an eight-band Dutch-made Philco radio that picked up stations from Cairo and Beirut broadcasting the latest news and musical programs from that part of the world as well as the commanding voice of a muezzin calling the hour of daily prayer, a recording of which, years later, he would give me as a present. Everyone adopted a hangdog look, even our neighbor tia Arminda, a cheerful Portuguese woman from Minho who met the most difficult moments with a per-

petual smile that seemed to split her face wide open—
even she stood closed-faced, hiding her buck teeth. I
hunkered down beside Samara, her damp hand in
mine, sharing a case of the cold sweats. Hindié recalled that Father was capable of leveling her with one
look, but tonight he looked at no one as he crossed
the room. As he disappeared alone into the night, Emilie began clapping and chattering, and pulled me
away from Samara to dance with her, and so there was
dancing and laughter without the shadow of my father
troubling the brightly lit house.

"I showed people to their places at the table, without
any idea if they planned on going to midnight mass,"
Hindié went on, smoking nervously, inhaling and ex-
haling practically simultaneously, the hand with the fan
quivering like the wings of a hummingbird.

Mama stopped dancing and led me to the table, insisting loudly that the guests stay for dinner. Many did.
Then, very unceremoniously, with the most natural
gesture in the world, she sat me at the head of the
table, in my father's customary place, and announced
that since her blouse was sopping wet from dancing she
was going to change and would be right back. She was
not gone long, but when she reappeared in the parlor
her face no longer had the boundlessly appealing look
of gleaming ivory bathed in light. People began to whisper among themselves and Hindié rushed to her
friend's side to try to help minimize embarrassment.

"She told me she felt sharp pangs in her head when
she walked into her bedroom," said Hindié. "Then

your mother changed the subject, and hurried off to get fruit juice for all the children, and whenever anyone complimented her on a particular dish she'd recite the recipe out loud in a flustered voice, remember?"

I do remember that she stayed right by my side, making sure I ate well even though I didn't feel like it. She popped food into Samara's mouth and daintily sampled the hors d'oeuvres herself, chatting all the while, asking Arminda if she'd heard from her relatives in Portugal, asking Sara Benemou when the synagogue was scheduled to open and whether tabouleh and esfiha with ground lamb were common in Rabat, and asking everyone, with an excited and all-inclusive look, whether they'd heard that Dorner was back in town.

"Dorner lived in Manaus six or seven years ago," said Emilie. "Then he went on a long trip through the jungle and went south to see some relatives."

"You were single back then," remarked Esmeralda.

"Single, lucky, and unlucky," added Emilie, her eyes searching for an oval picture frame on the white wall. "Dorner knew my husband and was a friend of my little brother Emir."

Emilie appeared almost breathless, and her nervous, tremulous voice sparked everyone's interest. But in the silence that followed, we all turned to the oval-framed photograph of a young man whose wide-eyed, adrift look obliged the observer to avert his or her gaze and search in vain for something else to look at, but there was nothing else on that white wall, there was no escaping that photograph.

"The other day I ran into Dorner at the Café Polar," said Esmeralda. "He seemed to be having a grand old time with some of the friends he left behind, and I heard him ask if they knew anyone who had gotten engaged or was celebrating a birthday this week. Sounds like he's back to stay."

Arminda pronounced Dorner both generous and learned but full of eccentricities. He collected everything you could think of and was interested in everything, just like the Commander, and he just loved to take people by surprise. Arminda rummaged around in her pocketbook and drew out a photograph, where we saw her smiling face, pale and astonished, at a window framed by hydrangeas.

"He caught me by surprise, all right," she laughed.

Emilie regretted not having invited him; the poor man had no family here and would be spending Christmas alone. She'd hardly finished proclaiming that outsiders were always welcome when we heard hand-clapping and a booming "Good evening and Merry Christmas to all!" The children laughed at the sight of his tall frame unceremoniously stumbling past the showcases and into the living room. He had red splotches on his clean-shaven face, and a box dangled from a strap wound around his fist and secured as firmly and greedily as a hawk secures its prey. "Your ears must be burning!" exclaimed Arminda in her Minho accent. Dorner greeted everybody one by one, leaning down to kiss the ladies' hands and tousle the children's hair. Then he positioned Arminda's hand so that the photograph hovered beside her face, unrolled the strap from his hand, and removed the camera from the box in one smooth, feline gesture. We heard the pop and were immediately plunged into the stupefying blindness of the flash, which turned everything dazzling white. When finally people and objects reappeared, the two Armindas were still smiling, undaunted and startled. The following week, when Dorner showed around the photograph of the woman's face beside the photograph of the woman's face, an old suspicion was put to rest: Arminda's perpetual smile was not a smile but a grimace acquired in childhood, as our neighbor Esmeralda had revealed to Hindié Conceição.

It wasn't just Arminda's family—all the neighbors wanted to know what had happened that Christmas Eve. It was widely suspected that Father had not slept at home and was still off somewhere without a trace. Dorner's late and unexpected visit had been a consolation to Emilie and avoided even greater embarrassment.

"Without that distraction," observed Hindié, "your mother would have gone on clutching you to her side, spitting out words and devouring food so as not to lose heart and give way to her despair, which she in fact did sometime in the wee hours long after the guests had gone. I arrived at the Parisian early the next morning to find the same mess as the night before."

A battalion of fire ants, attracted by the crumbs and the honey in the baklava, had invaded the showcases; the table was littered with a jumble of bones and fruit rinds, and the porcelain serving platters swarmed with flies. The rustic landscape embroidered on the table-cloth (a hunter beside a stream, his sights on a white-plumed bird, and a peacock whose fanned-out tail feathers filtered the sunlight) was splotched with grease and beverage stains. Since this was Anastácia's only day off—she would go visit relatives and not return until evening—Emilie herself would have to manage the cleanup, so that by late afternoon the Parisian would once more be a home and a shop instead of a chaotic space as disconcerting to customer as to guest.

"Anastácia was just leaving when I got there," said Hindié, "but she refused to tell me why the house was such a mess. She did say that Emilie had wandered the house at loose ends until sunup, hovering outside the children's door, throwing up for a time in the bath-room. She asked Anastácia to get her some glue, tooth-picks, and scissors. Her hands were trembling and her face was swollen, and before locking herself in her room, she whispered a few words in Anastácia's ear. I begged her to tell me what Emilie had said, but do you know what Anastácia replied? She said, 'I'd die first. The mistress said it was a secret.' Then, looking ex-tremely righteous and responsible, she added: 'I really must be going, it's getting late. Dona Emilie is in her room, go on in, I'm sure she's awake by now.' Actually, your mother had never slept. I found her sitting on the floor, and when she saw me she patted a spot on the carpet next to her and said hoarsely: 'I took the children to Esmeralda's for the day. Sit down right here and help me; there's more than enough to do.' The bedroom was in a complete uproar."

Hindié paused, ducked behind her fan, and leaned back in her chair. She remained silent for a moment: to jog her memory? to catch her breath? to tamp down the resentment that accompanied the memory of that day? Finally, without lowering the fan from her face, she ennumerated, in a voice heavy with anger and offense, all the plaster saints reduced to dust, wooden carvings barbarously broken, Our Lady of the Immaculate Conception smashed to bits and the Baby Jesus destroyed. The rare illuminated manuscripts Emilie had brought from the Iberian peninsula were still intact, as well as the mahogany oratory and the image of Our Lady of Lebanon; these at least had escaped Father's fury. The bedroom looked as though it had been ravaged by a cataclysm or a cyclone, or by a single scream from the All-Powerful Himself. Hindié peered at me over her fan as if I were an echo, a reverberation of paternal rage, as if time had taken a leap backward and at that instant she were sharing in Emilie's lamentations and I had disappeared after having profaned the bedroom. I hadn't said a word, meanwhile. My reaction must have been written on my face: surprise, interest, pain, commiseration. Why was she telling me all this? Not merely to state the case against my father, destroyer of nearly all the religious objects that nourished the two women day to day, but also to redeem herself for defying the word of the Prophet. I pictured Hindié and my mother sitting on the carpet with its design recalling the Door of the Sepulchre, with its rosettes and helixes, circles, squares, and triangles, and a delicate floral and geometrical motif inside a hexagon inscribed in a circle. Bent over the carpet collecting fragments of plaster and splinters of wood to reconstruct the saints' images, they didn't know (maybe only Father knew) that those designs symbolized the creation, the sun and moon, the cosmic progression of time and space, the cycle of the revolutions of earthly time, and eternity. Or that right in the center of the carpet, in a half-circle worn thin from the assiduous contact of a body bowed in prayer, there was a box or chest containing the Book of Revelation, represented by a small yellow square.

As Hindié described how the two women glued splinters together, retouched the statuettes' mantles and hair with pigment from fruit seeds and rinds, and hunted with lynx eyes for more lost shards of plaster in the carpet, I sat thinking, with a contained smile, about what had happened in the days following that Christmas Eve. Before then, religion had not caused serious dissension between my parents. Father accepted our celebrating Christian holidays and seemed tolerant of Emilie's religious fervor, though he clearly disdained her incessant prayers. He simply shut his eyes to all the images and statues of saints and steered clear of the little sewing room where the two women folded and cut rectangles of tracing paper to make colorful miniature saints for the first communion of the orphans at Nossa Senhora Auxiliadora school.

The restoration of the holy objects took up the whole day. Touch-ups with homemade paint and crack marks notwithstanding, the statues were back on their wooden pedestals or in their niches by late afternoon.

"I was totally exhausted," said Hindié, "but it was as if your mother were delirious or suffering from tunnel vision. She still had the energy to tidy up the parlor, fumigate the showcases and damp corners of the house, and arrange some flowers for the table. Even though she did most of this herself, I was dead on my feet by the time Esmeralda brought you children home. My head was reeling, and I had terrible eyestrain after almost ten hours sitting on the carpet gathering up those tiny pieces. On my way out, I saw your father approaching in the distance. Under his arm he carried the radio and the water pipe; behind him trooped Anastácia with his cloth bundle and packages. Had she run into him by chance? Had your parents argued during the night? I don't know, because Emilie said nothing and I thought better of asking. But the following Christmas Emilie asked me very discreetly to leave the butchering to your Uncle Emílio, that wise angel who'd had a premonition of disaster and absented himself from the Christmas festivities."

Hindié never found out that Anastácia had served as mediator between my parents, or that Emilie had commissioned her to find Father at all costs and bring him

back by dinnertime. Or that in the midst of all her torment that night, Emilie did not forget to set aside a
plate of food, a tray of sweets and dried fruit, and a bowl
of guava compote for him. Emilie's whispered message
to Anastácia had been that the wrath of a hot-blooded
man can be tempered by good food and affection.

"When it comes to calming my husband's dog temper, those are two powerful weapons," she announced.

I learned later that Anastácia had spent the whole
day searching for Father, finally locating him at the
Floating City talking to some friends from the interior.
He had slept at the home of a friend he'd met on the
river Purus: a pink-and-green hut on stilts, surrounded
by caladiums, white lilies, and jungle plants potted in
kerosene cans. He was sitting in the middle of a group
of men intently listening to a strange voice on the radio
sing a song that provoked ripples of laughter.

"As soon as he saw me, he scrambled to his feet and
asked about your mother," said Anastácia.

"What did you say?"

"I told him that she had been waiting for him for
dinner since yesterday, and that the bedroom rug was
shining like the morning sun."

AND SO Anastácia and Father arrived home together.
Anastácia headed straight for the kitchen, but Emilie
called out to her:

"Take the children's dinner to their room."

From this we understood that we were to spend the

rest of the evening in our bedroom. Samara clung to me like a vine, peering sideways at Father, who rounded the showcases and passed like a stranger within a few meters of our bedroom door. Even so, we said goodnight in unison, in tiny voices we could hardly get out of our mouths. Emilie's answer was to come kiss us goodnight. She was perfumed as never before, and when she tousled my hair I noticed she was wearing the sapphire ring so remarked upon in conversations about jewelry from the East; her hair was pulled back in a knot at the back of her neck, accentuating her smooth forehead, which smelled of amber and was the color of almonds. I remember that I didn't have much appetite for the leftovers from Christmas Eve dinner, and that for a good part of the night I lay with my ears perked up listening to the movements on the other side of the wall. I was afraid that Father was about to become as ferocious and invincible as Antar in the Arab legend and attack the woman who kissed me every night just before I slipped into sleep. The hours were long and tense. I expected a reprisal at any moment, revenge of some sort, the crushing sound of a solid wall being demolished. I fell asleep with these disturbing thoughts running through my head, my hand entwined with Samara's, who always went to bed with a lace ribbon in her hair.

The next morning as I walked through the store on my way out to school I saw Father furtively placing the saints' images in the cabinet reserved for bridal wreaths. I thought nothing of it at the time, imagining that Emi-

lie had asked him to put them away, to protect them
from the fungus and termites that changed the color of
plaster and rotted wood during the rainy months. But
when I came home from school at noon, the house was
turned upside down and everyone was busy looking for
the statues. There was deep satisfaction, if not glee, on
Father's face as he watched Emilie's anguish—her wild
expression and croaking voice, followed by the sound of
fists pounding the table, then the wall. She pursed her
lips, she sputtered and fumed, she asked Anastácia if
any strangers had been in her room or if by chance she
had taken the saints off to be cleaned. I waited until
siesta time to tell my mother about the statues' profane
altar. She could hardly believe it, but there they were. In
addition to covering me with kisses she decided to award
me a monthly allowance of twenty réis, so I could buy
candy and other treats on the street. The following day
the episode was repeated, and on and on for a week: in
the morning, while Emilie was at the market, Father
would make off with the saints and then in the afternoon I'd get them back for her. Emilie accepted this
game in good humor, but not without plotting revenge.
She waited patiently for the month of June. On the
morning of the twenty-seventh, the doors of the Parisian
were locked and bolted. House and shop alike became a
dark prison in which Father stumbled blindly looking
for the Four Angels of Glorification and the Twenty-
eight Lunar Houses where the Alphabet and Man in his
Plenitude reside. And while Father had locked the house
up tight, isolating it from the world, he didn't raise the

expected protest, nor did he appeal to anyone to help him find the Book. It was only Father and Anastácia who were isolated, actually, because Samara and I were at school. Returning from the market, Emilie found the doors bolted and banged the iron door knocker in the shape of a tiny hand. No response from inside. When I came home and stood, openmouthed, before the dark facade, she put her arms around me and said with a triumphant smile:

"You know how rattled your father gets on fast days, my dear."

Without understanding what she meant, I knew something strange was going on in the Parisian. For me, it was a Friday like any other; it made no sense for us to be stranded outside staring at five locked doors, watching my exhilarated mother whack that little iron hand against the massive wooden door. Emilie led us out to the sidewalk, sat us down under a chestnut tree, opened a straw basket, and offered us some fruit. Then she removed a notebook and pencil from my knapsack and began writing, her hand moving easily and slowly in a cursive scrawl, sowing among the black lines a dancing script, enigmatic as hieroglyphics. She wrote a message three lines long, tore the sheet from the notebook, folded it in half, and asked me to slip it under the door. A few minutes later, Anastácia Socorro appeared in the main doorway shaking her head. Then she pointed her right index finger at her ear and moved it in a circular motion, while her other index finger pointed furiously to the Parisian. The sight of her skinny body framed by the dark doorway tracing circle after circle reduced us to peals of laughter, which only subsided once we plunged into the darkness ourselves and heard a deep and melodious voice.

"That means he found it," said Emilie curtly. Only then did we realize that she had hidden the Book, and that Father had darkened and locked up the house to make certain that no human creature would see anything until the Book was found.

The voice filled the air completely as we threw open all the doors and windows. People passing on the sidewalk paused to listen and tried to peer inside the house to discover the origin of the sound. They stared at us, as if to ask: Who's the ventriloquist? From what wall or cave does that voice issue? It came from the bedroom, where a body weak from days of fasting was strong enough to bawl the last day's prayers. A fascination began growing in me that day, a boundless curiosity about the three lines Emilie had scrawled in my notebook and about my father's voice. Even though I was used to hearing that strange language occasionally, I thought it was only spoken by old people; or at least I thought that adults didn't speak like children. Little by little I realized that people used their arms more when they spoke that language, and there were times when I intuited concepts through their gestures. One night when I was eavesdropping on the conversation, I asked if they were talking about our new neighbor. They said they were talking about me, about my curiosity, and the fact that I liked to hang around and listen to a language I didn't understand. That night, my mother sat down beside me on my bed before kissing me goodnight and whispered that the following Saturday we would begin to study the "alifebata" together. She told me that her grandmother had taught her to read and write before she even went to school. As a way of explaining her apprenticeship in the mother tongue, she told me succinctly how Salma, my great-grandmother, had died at the age of 105. With no reluctance or fear, I devoutly believed those words that set my eyes on fire, as the celestial abyss was made manifest in the space of an open window, for from that limitless precipice winged and illuminated beings left their dwelling place to float alongside the deathbed.

"There are more than twenty angels and they came with the little children," Salma had whispered before closing her eyes. And Emilie recounted the story of Salma and the angels so many times that I ended up dreaming about them.

The following day, both story and dream streamed through my thoughts like water from two stormy rivers mingling to create a third. I let myself be pulled along by that wild flood, thinking, too, about shapes on the page, the handwriting that looked like marks made by a bird's wings as it tumbled in a mirror of sand, and about my father's stern voice, more lucid than lugubrious, a polished and placid voice that I tried to imitate as soon as I learned the Arabic alphabet, before even pronouncing a single word in that language, which, though familiar, sounded the most foreign of all foreign languages.

I waited for Saturday, anxious for the hours and minutes to evaporate, my attention quadrupled whenever Father let slip a phrase in that other language. On Saturday, before we sat down for our midday meal, the words he'd just said, which he always said before every meal, gushed from my mouth almost involuntarily. Samara shot me an incredulous look and let out a peal of laughter, which she choked back immediately at the silence of our parents. Father turned to me, and his gaze, which lasted for just a spasm, flared like the eyes of a newborn blinded by the first explosion of light.

My first Arabic lessons consisted of little excursions into the veiled and secluded nooks and crannies of the Parisian, rooms and cubicles lit dimly by skylights: the dead spaces of architecture. Those little rooms scared me, and I didn't understand why my initial contact with the language should consist of visiting them. After opening the doors and turning on the lights, Emilie would point to an object and slowly articulate a word that seemed to burst in her throat; the syllables, jumbled at first, soon sounded distinct enough that I could repeat them several times. Not a single object escaped this nominative quest, from store mechandise to personal possessions: porcelain melting pots, pillows embroidered with arabesques, dainty crystal flasks containing camphor and benjamin, leather sandals, chandeliers made from milky glass orbs, Spanish fans, bolts of cloth, and a collection of perfume bottles forming a caravan of smells from musk to amber that I breathed in as I repeated the correct name for each. After our pilgrimage through the rooms and showcases in the store, we would sit down at the living-room table, and Emilie wrote down each word I'd learned, indicating whether each letter appeared near the beginning, middle, or end of the alphabet. Then I copied it all, straining to write from right to left, forming each letter innumerable times, filling page after page of ruled paper. At afternoon's end, I'd run to show Father my work, which he would correct while Emilie disappeared into the room next to his, which was hers alone to enter. Emilie's teaching followed no method, order, or sequence. Somewhere along my haphazard apprenticeship I began to get a notion, perhaps intuitively, of the contour of the "alifebata," until finally the backbone of the new language was revealed: the lunar and solar letters, the subtleties of grammar and phonetics that glit-' tered in each object exposed in the showcases or hidden away in the shadowy rooms. I spent five or six years practicing this diaphanous game halfway between pronunciation and orthography, sifting and distinguishing sounds, painstakingly gaining the hand control to represent them on paper, as if the pencil point were a chisel artfully furrowing a slab of marble that would little by little become populated by minuscule writhing and spiraling creatures who aspired to the form of snails, gouges, scimitars, and one lonely beast that, when brought into contact with the back of the teeth, the tongue could thrust out in a sudden spasm from between half-open lips: a Phoenician fish.

FROM THE TIME I was small I inhabited one language in school and on the streets and another at the Parisian. Sometimes it felt as if I were living two distinct lives. I knew I'd been elected Interlocutor Number One among Emilie's children: because I was first? because that meant I was closer to her memories, to the ancestral world where everything or almost everything revolved around Tripoli, mountains, cedars, fig trees and vines, sheep, Junieh, and Ebrin? But that's not what was perplexing; what really intrigued me was Mama's solitary excursion after we finished our lessons. Invariably she'd disappear into the room that fascinated me for the mere fact of its being an inviolable space, inaccessible even to Father, who closed his eyes completely to her comings and goings from that hideaway, loaded down with stuff, piles of papers covered with words and expressions we'd studied on Saturday afternoons. It was only when we moved to the new house that this sanctuary of secrets was dismantled. Moving brings revelations and leaves mysteries; on the way from one space to another something is revealed and even the contents of a secret document may become public. Emilie placed the things from her secret room in the locked trunk and carried it herself the entire two city blocks to the new house. I followed at a distance. Whenever she paused to rest along the way, I hid behind a tree. She would never have forgiven me if she had discovered me watching every step of the way to make sure she didn't stumble and fall, dropping her world onto the sidewalk. The minute she arrived safely at the new house I began wondering, Where would she hide that weighty thing full of ancient secrets and inaccessible belongings?

ONE MORNING WHEN Emilie was off doing her daily marketing I ransacked my parents' bedroom. I must have been nearly twenty years old at the time and I remember that the house was truly enormous. There were four of us children then, so a larger house had been needed to accommodate the family that, for better or worse, had been accumulating little ones at six-year intervals: you, your brother, and Soraya Ângela. I turned my parents' bedroom inside out trying to locate the perfect hiding place for a key; I looked between cracks in the shutters, under upholstered cushions, beneath loose floorboards, inside pillows, and even under the mattress they had been sleeping on together for decades. It was a meticulous search stretching over several mornings one August that, today, seems a century ago. The search only paid off when, my patience wearing thin, I began shaking things and turning them upside down, including a souvenir piece of Cedar of Lebanon in the shape of a tree. The cone-shaped top section had bark wrapped around and glued to it, while the base was entirely smooth except for a tiny cedar tree carved in relief, just slightly larger than a human eye. Later I understood why Emilie sometimes prolonged her afternoon rest in the hammock, with a nostalgic eye on the piece of cedar perched on top of the dresser; I discovered that the miniature tree on the base of this knicknack I had assumed to be entirely solid was actually the secret to its opening, and that in the heart of the cedar, slipped into a thin slot in the wood, lay two keys. One of the keys unlocked the mastodon wardrobe, the doors flinging open to reveal Emilie's intimate world to me for the first time. I remember feeling both embarrassed and entranced by the sight of so many things I'd never laid my eyes on in the Parisian; but embarrassment and enchantment almost always take hold when we trespass on another's privacy.

The wardrobe was filled with luxurious garments, many of them with magnificent brocade work. Hidden away in the dark, abandoned and unused, these clothes seemed to allude to a body from a different time, one that walked on different soil and braved the seasons of a far-off place; I tried to imagine Emilie's body in these exotic clothes, which I could only partially appreciate in the dark corners of a cupboard. I envisioned scenes from her adolescence, the same way I ponder from this vantage point in time my successive incursions into the interior of the wardrobe, searching for objects, searching for words.

I returned morning after morning because, once I

had opened the wardrobe and the trunk inside it, I couldn't help lingering over the vision of the clock laid on its back, almost completely filling the trunk, which was lined with velvet, also black, like a ship laid to rest and forgotten on the bottom of the ocean. Behind the glass door I could see the letters Hindié had told me about. Violating the correspondence hidden inside the clock would imply penetrating a place in time far from the present. As unaware as I may have been, I was playing the foolish, delicate—even irrational—game that consists of uncovering someone's past, exploring unknown zones of time and space: Tripoli, 1898; Ebrin, 1917; Beirut, 1920; Chipre, Trieste, Marseilles, Recife, and Manaus, 1924. These were dates and places mentioned sporadically by Hindié, and I wanted to link them firmly to Emilie's life, I wanted to discover the secrets preserved in the belly of that dark box. One morning, quite a long time after my first discovery, having on numerous occasions postponed the turning of the smaller key, the mental caressing of the smooth, glassy surface, the visual probing of the angles of shadow, I decided to open the glass door, to penetrate the inside of the clock, where face, hands, numerals, pendulum, everything was covered with objects. The first to catch my eye were two gold bracelets, thin hoops joined by almost invisible knots; actually, it didn't seem to me to be knots that made the two bracelets one, but a kind of magical interweaving, an inexplicable articulation that, upon handling, inspired curiosity and amazement. You must remember that bracelet Emilie wore twined around her forearm like a golden tattoo. On another venture into the trunk—to reread a letter—another pair of bracelets appeared, like a new ring appearing on the body of a snake. It took a while for me to relate the number of bracelets to the number of children. I never discovered the origin of those thin hoops that secretly reproduced in their bed on the clock. There was no mention of them in the letters, and several times I stopped myself from asking Emilie about it; my surprising restraint convinced me once and for all that there are powerful secrets or indecipherable riddles that certain people carry with them to the grave. It was after my youngest brother was born that Emilie started wearing the bracelets. By that time, I had thoroughly examined the recesses of the trunk and the clock buried inside it: I'd seen the white linen nun's habit spotted with yellow stains and mildew, the signs of abandon. I never dared touch it, or the pleated wimple, each carefully folded and placed one on top of the other, like the shadow of a face and the shape of a body protected by the clock face. They had clearly lay undisturbed for a long time, since an infinitely complicated and incredibly compact web, which looked as if it were still growing by the day, lay on top of the stains and mold; perhaps these signs of permanence and disuse, remoteness and secrecy, were what prevented me from disturbing the habit worn for so short a time at Ebrin. I finally did manage to piece together the details of that episode in her life, though, as well as others both in Lebanon and Manaus, thanks to the letters wedged in under the disk-shaped weight of the pendulum tucked inside its wooden box.

Deciphering the crabbed handwriting was a wearisome task. Written in classical Arabic, and always signed V.B., the letters spanned years and years, sometimes interrupted for intervals of several months. During these periods of silence, the thread of the story would be lost and I'd have a lot of trouble with the handwriting in the next batch of letters, skipping over whole sentences and cursing the difficult vocabulary, like a reader led to a dead end by undecipherable signs. The intermittence of the correspondence and the difficulty of deciphering much of it permitted only the blindest groping toward a monologue, or not even a half-voice, a text with no spark, which made for a faltering reader. I attacked the most obscure passages of the letters with the help of intuition: a potentially useful resource in confronting such a lurching narrative without the assistance of a dictionary, though for better or worse I did consult the notebooks that were stacked up beside the letters; perusing her notes, I came across many references to our Saturday lessons, and I was amazed to see that the vocabulary we had compiled was quite vast. I also found some prayers she'd written out in French—so many Ave Marias, in fact, that I imagined Emilie must have copied out litanies on her nights of despair when she couldn't bring herself to pray. How many times had I surprised her intoning hymns, the palms of her hands crossed over her chest and her eyes darting from one Bible to another; I'm convinced that was why she could readily learn psalms in Portuguese, though her face would narrow when sometimes the crossing from one language to the other felt strange and disloyal, as if the holy words were being smashed against the rocks, rendering them tedious or devoid of meaning. This must have been an important issue for Emilie because V.B. mentions it in several letters, and she transcribes a passage from the French Bible, asking her friend to translate it into Portuguese. I noticed when I visited Emir's grave that the Bible quotation there appeared in both languages, chiseled on the headstone beneath the photograph of a young figure.

The name Emir was almost never spoken at mealtimes or in the conversations enlivened by tokes on the water pipe, sips of anise liqueur, and bold moves in backgammon. We children were not allowed to be part of these parties that lasted through the night and always ended up on the patio with the fountain, lit by a bluish light. There was a moment when the old, worn-out subjects, tired from so many repetitions, gave way to confidences and regrets, sometimes drowned out by the language of the birds and interspersed with exclamations. It was as if morning—like an intruder silencing the heated voices of night—had the power to dissipate the festive mood, toning down even the most extravagant talkers, calling them to the business that begins at dawn. Occasionally, however, the signs of morning would have no effect. I'd awake to earsplitting howls and terrible wailing, to the sounds of mockery and the bawling of animals as they witnessed the agony

of some sheep with a pet name who'd been hand-fed by
Emilie. I'd run to my parents' bedroom, peek through
the cracks in the shutters as the blood spurted from the
animal's neck and dripped down the eyes and onto the
curly white coat, turning it the dubious color of that
dusky stain in the middle of the patio in the new morning. It wasn't until the last drop of blood had run out
that it was time to cut and dress the animal. Emilie
pulled the organs out with her bare hands, placing the
parts to be eaten later on a slab of cedar and throwing
the rest to the animals. And while a storm took shape
around her—chickens, dogs, cats, and monkeys wran-
gling for sheep's guts—she calmly cleaned and washed
the liver, seasoning it with salt, pepper, and mint. The
backgammon boards were removed from the table and
some player made a point of remembering that the next
throw would be his.

Emilie always helped Anastácia serve the paper-thin
dough, folded like a stack of delicate silk handkerchiefs,
a basket of Indian figs, genipaps, biribás, pineapple,
and watermelon, and a fired-clay bowl with poppies
from the garden set around the edges and clusters of
pitomba berries, strings of wild maracujá, and other
fruit bitter enough to make your body shiver and your
face wince. But Anastácia's face was wincing for another reason; after setting the table, she withdrew to one of
the back rooms so she wouldn't have to watch the glut-
tonous ritual. In the center of a patio lit by the equato-
rial sun, a group of men and women reenacted the
age-old gastronomical custom of eating raw sheep's liv-

er with their bare hands. To me, riveted at my parents'
bedroom window, it didn't look like an animal sacrifice
or a barbarous ritual at all, but an awesome novelty, an
exotic feast, utterly alien to the habitual rhythm of the
house.

Unlike the usual antiseptic mode of eating, there was
extravagance and deep pleasure in the way they gave
themselves to their hunger, in their deliberate surrender to the meat, hands grasping and thrusting to
mouth pieces of raw liver and bread passed from hand
to hand, chunks ripped off by fingers dripping grease
and zaartar. Someone would sing the latest tune from
Cairo; someone else would recite one of Attar's mystical poems, or recall the "Song of the Rose," the "Car-
nation," the "Anemone," concluding with a quotation
from the "Song of Jasmine" that says despair is a mis-
take. There would be praises for the seasonings, the
semolina cakes with almonds and honey, and the rose
petal compote, which everyone breathed in slowly before tasting. Some, worried that they would not be invited back for Saturday night—when the leg of roast
lamb with dates would be served—awaited anxiously
the moment of leave-taking, hoping that Father would
quote the line about God permitting him to open the
doors to them for tomorrow's dinner.

These gatherings continued in the new house, but it
was while we lived in the Parisian that I first became
aware of their existence. Conversation was exclusively
in Arabic, except for greetings to some acquaintance
who happened to drop by, or the visit of a neighbor

from another country, like Américo and his family, the Benemous from Morocco, and Gustav Dorner, the young man from Hamburg. All of them were very friendly with Emilie, and the last, in addition to a friend, became my confidant.

It was through Dorner that I was introduced to the first library in my life. It consisted of eight walls of books, which I visited only some years later, fortunately, because I'm sure it would have been overwhelming to the point of inhibiting my newly developing habit of reading. Dorner's voice was as sober as his name, and he spoke a very refined Portuguese, with almost no accent, which was disconcerting to natives because the only reason he couldn't be taken for a native of Amazonas was his appearance. He was taller and blonder than the other Germans in the city, and wore clothes peculiar for the time: Bermuda shorts, a white collarless shirt, and two-tone leather shoes with no laces or socks. A black box hung from his waist, tied to a leather belt; from a distance it looked like a holster or canteen. His dexterity in getting the Hasselblad out of the case was impressive as he dashed off to capture an image on the streets, in homes or churches, at the port, in the park, or in the middle of the river. In addition, Dorner possessed an enviable memory: the whole of his shared past here in Manaus as well as the details of life in his own country pulsed through the torrent of words from his thundering voice, pounding the silence of the entire city block. But memory was also evoked through images; he called himself an implacable pursuer of "mo-

ments aflame with humanity and singular nature-
scapes of the Amazon." He had been amassing this
"heap of life's surprises" for some time: a portrait of a
monk, a beggar, a fisherman, Indians who lived on the
edge of the jungle, songbirds, flowers, and crowds of
people.

I'm sure you and your brother remember Dorner. I
don't know if you were ever one of his students, but
surely you know how distracted he was. Sometimes I
thought it was a strategy, a way to evade the people and
the reality surrounding him; everything he saw was
framed in the viewfinder of his camera. Once I told
him that I thought the lenses of his Hassel, his eye-
glasses, and his blue pupils comprised a unique optical
system. My slightly aberrant comparisons didn't irritate
him; he simply replied that when he looked in the camera he saw his own face. And that on certain hot
nights, returning home from a walk through the deserted city, he would suddenly come across this other face
illuminated and inlaid in a square of glass, where the
Hassel sat during the night, spending the wee hours in
the warmth of a lamp, basking in dry, artificial heat—to
prevent fungus, preserve the clarity of the lens and the
view: the triumph of transparency.

Dorner took a picture of Emir in the center of the
bandstand in the park across from the police station. It
was the last photograph of Emir, taken moments before
his final solitary walk to the docks, a walk that ended at
the bottom of the river. Dorner himself told me the
story of the photograph years later, trying with mea-

sured words to avoid betraying an excruciating fact that I had already intuited from reading the letters of Virginie Boulad. The photo revealed what Dorner couldn't: the tense face of a body walking aimlessly or in circles. One of Emir's hands was in his pants pocket; the other gently caressed an orchid so rare that Dorner couldn't even guess at the depth of his friend's despair.

During one of our last times together, Dorner recalled that morning and showed me several notebooks in which he'd transcribed some of his conversations with Father.

DORNER

I N THOSE DAYS I made my living with my Hassel-blad, and I also did a little work with a Pathé motion-picture camera. I took pictures of God and everything else in this city worn down by loneliness and decadence. Lots of people wanted their pictures taken, as if suspending time in that way would protect them from the disenchantment of the era and create a small, phantasmagoric world, a world of images, sheltering whole families gathered in their extravagant gardens or on the deck of some steamer in the port of Manaus to sit before the lens.

The morning I spotted Emir on the bandstand in the square I was on my way to the home of the Alhers, one of those families that at the turn of the century were capable of influencing the mood and destiny of almost the entire population, urban and otherwise, because they controlled river navigation and thus food distribution. My work for the morning was to take a series of Alher family portraits and then to return to my darkroom to develop and print the film from one of my trips to the Rio Branco waterfall, where I'd made a photographic record of the extraordinary flowers there—none of them as rare, however, as the orchid Emir was displaying in his left hand. I was especially struck by its color, an exaggerated purplish red, almost violet. Maybe because I was so intensely focused on the flower I didn't immediately register his odd expression, the vacant look of someone who no longer recognizes familiar faces. I invited Emir to lunch with me at the French restaurant in town; he responded by mumbling something enigmatic, which I took to be a refusal. It was clear that he wanted to withdraw—from me and from everyone else, and that his very will to live was tied up somehow with that orchid sprouting from his hand.

As I photographed the Alhers, past conversations I'd had with Emir came to mind. He spoke in a kind of gibberish; I always felt as if I were listening to a North African storyteller, someone with an incredible gift for convincing people with his voice, rather than his words, since much of what he said was incomprehensible. His habitual solitary strolls were equally baffling. He'd leave the Hotel Fenícia very early, rouse a boatman down by the local market to row him across to the other side of the waterway, *igarapé* Educandos, and then continue on foot all the way downtown, past street after narrow street lined with tumbledown houses. I know because I followed him a couple of times. Emir wasn't like a lot of the other immigrants. He didn't hole up in the interior defying wild animals and incessant fevers, caught in the constant coming and going between Manaus and the web of rivers; he simply didn't possess the rage and determination of those who arrived young and poor and utterly dedicated to the idea of having an empire to show for themselves by the end of their tormented lives. Emir retreated from everything, he had a lost look about him, like someone who talks to you, looks you in the face, but it's as if there's no one behind his eyes. Those walks of his were another thing that interested me about him, the way he strolled the neighborhood filled with cheap boarding-houses, past the Traveler's Hotel, never stopping, never focusing on anyone, merely braving the silence at the end of night or the sudden scream or laugh or flash of light exploding in a bedroom window. Emir's life seemed reduced to these predawn strolls: after crossing the igarapé he'd walk to Dom Pedro II Square and turn down the street lined with big warehouses, where he'd see masts and keels and high smokestacks and hear the deep-pitched whistle of the *Hildebrand*, bringing passengers from Liverpool, Leixões, and the islands of Madeira; maybe he even knew the ship's destination: New York, Los Angeles, some port city in the other hemisphere, nostalgia for overseas. The Ahler family stood carefully positioned on the other side of the viewfinder, arm-in-arm beside a grimy statue, but all I could see was Emir's face, the orchid balanced in his hand, and the ring on one of his fingers: a gift he'd proudly showed me one day, a keepsake of his love affair in Marseilles.

I didn't get much done in the darkroom. I just couldn't focus on images of waterfalls, Indians, and rare plants. A strange feeling had settled over me, a premonition or sense of foreboding, so I gave up and went out, my camera over my shoulder. It was already beginning to drizzle by the time I got to the Ville de Paris for lunch. I noticed an unusual buzzing among the passersby milling about on the sidewalk, and then sirens cut through the midday lull. There was a bit of a commotion in the restaurant. I sat down at the only empty table, then immediately changed my mind and rushed out the door, unaware whether I was walking fast or running, but following my intuition back to where I'd last seen Emir. The square was deserted. Then I remembered that beside the bronze sentinels on the sidewalk outside the barracks stood a pair of human sentries, timid shadows of the gigantic metal ones. After wondering momentarily if it was worth the time, I hurried off toward the barracks and called to them loudly, asking if by chance they had seen Emir. I lost about three minutes between crossing the square and my brief exchange with the sentry. His reply had the ring of the inevitable: A young man in a white suit?

Yes, he looked like he was talking to a flower. He walked away from the bandstand, heading that way, slowly, and disappeared.

The soldier pointed me in the direction Emir had gone, and as soon as the port came into view I noticed that one corner of the floating dock was jammed with people. Even from a distance I could make out the divers: two black shapes hovering in the blurry drizzle. The news spread like an epidemic, the many conflicting versions of which drove Emilie from laughter to tears and back again many times. The two security guards on duty gave contradictory reports regarding the man swallowed by the waters of the Rio Negro. Neither one had seen him come through the main gate but admitted he could easily have gone around behind the Customs Building and past the waterfront warehouse without being noticed. One of them claimed repeatedly that he'd seen a young man dressed in white at the edge of the dock.

"He was so still and so close to the water he looked like a marble statue floating above the surface," the man told a circle of onlookers.

But the other guard shook his head no and insisted that both men were too hungry and exhausted to see straight, their stomachs growling and their eyelids heavy.

"Besides, it's an impossible time of day," he said apologetically. "Made even worse by this drizzle and hazy sun. Your eyes can't make up their mind what they're seeing."

I was staring into the mirror of water shattered by fine rain when he said it: "Your eyes can't make up their mind what they're seeing." That's when I realized I'd left my Hasselblad at the restaurant, and as that reality began to sink in so did the certainty that Emir would not be found alive. Until that instant I had still been trying to believe the more hopeful rumors, my ears alert to each attempt to reconstruct my friend's path. I watched the successive forays of the divers impassively, the last spark of hope having faded with the realization that I'd left my camera behind. Even Emilie and Uncle Emílio remarked on my thunderstruck expression. My face felt utterly blank, as if I were blindfolded, disconnected from my body, like the vertigo following sudden blindness. The next thing I remember is Emilie's voice, and I could hear the great effort it took to demand over and over "What? What? Where?" Her questions resounded like hammer blows or warnings built of repetition: words and intonation exploding in fatal splinters of sound. As Emilie spoke, without looking at anyone, hands clasped over her ears and head thrown wildly back, the solid ring of people around the two guards melted and all eyes turned to her. Curious onlookers who had been gossiping among themselves hushed to a murmur and then fell silent, just as Emilie's words dissolved into a wail incomprehensible to everyone but her brother, struggling to hold her in his arms. The force of his grip unleashed a series of strange contortions; their bodies seemed to be struggling against something beyond themselves. After a few seconds, Emilie slumped forward, containing her movements, and froze in the shape of a mollusk, crouched on the metal platform.

The first whistle reverberated weakly, almost imperceptible; those closest to Emilie couldn't hear it above her wailing. I looked at the edge of the dock and saw the divers, their faces visible through the glass of their black masks, one man's arm pointing to the horizon. And then I heard a gentle flutelike sound, which seemed to be coming from a white smear that looked as if it were glued to the line of treetops but would dive now and then into the rays of the sun, or vanish in the haze of drizzle and reappear as a pure and luminous body, either motionless or moving so slowly it was impossible to tell if it were approaching us or drifting farther from port. Seen from a distance, wrapped in light and water, the white blur was like a living tableau, a slightly changeable painting: a watery horizon foggy and sunny at the same time, and the glint of a curved white blade drifting like an arc of light between sky and water.

The apparition on the horizon had gone unnoticed by the people around me. Emilie and her brother were still in their cocoon dance, one body covering the other, the crowd's running murmur breaking the silence as people watched, perplexed, having forgotten the drowned man, the search, the reason we were gathered there. It wasn't until I stepped off the other end of the dock, on my way down the gangway, that I heard the whistle again, clearer now, as if the sound were alien to the white on the horizon and issued from the haze itself: a whistle from space.

Hurrying back to the restaurant, I dodged several people who had clearly already heard the news. That's life in the provinces: a friend disappears, and a morbid atmosphere immediately falls over the city. First there are the indiscreet questions, then the perverse, lunatic insinuations about the victim—before we've even accepted the loss of a friend, our feelings still hovering between hope for his survival and mounting nostalgia, until we find ourselves in a kind of secret communion, a silent conversation with the past. Not without a certain regret, I wondered why I hadn't brought Emir with me to the sitting at the Ahlers' instead of just taking a picture of him with the orchid and leaving him to wander, dazed, one step from disaster. This image of Emir, still alive in my memory, was registered on film in the camera I'd left in the Ville de Paris. The owner of the restaurant had put the Hasselblad aside and was waiting anxiously. He bombarded me with questions and various confused hypotheses—a shipwreck, an explosion, all kinds of disaster scenarios. When I could finally get a word in edgewise, I began telling him what really had happened. I had no idea I was speaking German until he grabbed me by the arm and yelled: "Hey! What are you doing, talking to yourself?"

A similar thing happened over the following nights, in scattered, terribly unsettling dreams. I'd bolt upright, terrified, in the middle of the night and then toss and turn for hours, tormented not by fleeting images but by unintelligible dialogue, irretrievably lost. I'd dream that Emir and I were standing at the end of a dock before a thick dense curtain of drizzle at a time of day marked by silence. Our words didn't so much add up to a conversation as a hodgepodge of enigmas spoken by dissonant voices, because we each spoke our respective native tongues, which were no more than meaningless sounds to the other, words passing through an invisible prism, pure melody carried on a warm wind, noise cast into the air and swallowed by the fog: the incessant drizzle in dreams. How to understand oneself in this desperate attempt to understand the other? The anguish of incomprehension would suddenly wake me, and the rest of the night would crawl by, heavy and slow, as I painstakingly retrieved phrases from my dreams, trying to reconstruct the dialogue, remember sounds.

By two weeks after Emir's disappearance, the dreams had almost stopped. The last one coincided with the news that his body had been found at the bottom of an igarapé where not long before lovers had floated by in small boats or canoes with white canopies to shield them from the sun. It was Lobato, an Indian your father met before he married Emilie, who had found Emir's body. Your father was neither friendly nor scornful toward those close to the land; he showed a glacial indifference to everyone, including his children, as you know. He was devoted to keeping track of the merchandise, polishing the showcases, and, above all, chanting his prayers in some private Cave of Hira, in the recesses of the house or store.

"The doctors around here can hardly diagnose the

living! Why should I believe they can identify someone by examining a skeleton's teeth?" asked Emilie, unconvinced, before she had seen the body.

Your mother's disbelief was really quite unreasonable, since height, build, and everything else about the remains found in the river were unmistakably like her brother. None of this could persuade her, though, especially after she read a piece by a journalist claiming the body might be one of the many soldiers killed in the bloody skirmish of 1910 between state and federal troops.

"Every year at this time when the water is low, a body floats up and catches the public's attention," read the *Jornal do Comércio*. The publication of this fanciful article had begun to sow seeds of doubt in others' minds as well, when your father showed up one day with irrefutable evidence that dispelled all speculation as to the identity of the victim and, in a way, sealed Emilie's affective fate. I can still see the grim look on his face, his tall, thin, slightly stoop-shouldered frame, and his huge, flat hands. He walked into the house where Emilie was living with Emílio, introduced himself in Arabic and Portuguese, and declined the invitation to sit down because he was pressed for time. We other guests withdrew to the far side of the room. To my knowledge, no one had any idea why he had come. He removed a small box from his pocket, placed it in his upturned palm, and offered it to Emilie. The very moment he opened his mouth to speak, Emilie covered her face with her hands and stammered something I couldn't understand, just as I didn't understand your father's reply, spoken in that solemn voice he would have to his dying day.

They were married a few months after Emir's funeral. Needless to say, your father declined to attend the funeral, just as he did years later, when Emilie's parents died on the very same day in distant Recife. I had left Manaus by then, but I heard that her parents passed away when you were still a baby; it must have been hard for you suddenly to be without Emilie for several weeks. Your father refused to go, claiming he couldn't leave the Parisian in the hands of strangers, but he did allow Emilie to take a steamer to visit her parents' grave. Emílio went with her. In Manaus, he frequently accompanied her to the cemetery and to church. No one in your family ever asked me if I was religious, but I always imagined that they secretly disapproved of me—a foreigner living in the jungle with Indians who had never been inside a church but could recite a Hail Mary in Nhengatu.

Your parents were both fervently religious. Before they got married, they made a pact to respect the other's faith and to let their children opt for one or the other or none at all.

"All you have to do is look at the architecture of their places of worship to see the difference between the two religions," said your father in the midst of an explanation of the Prophet's genealogical tree one late afternoon in the Parisian. It was hard to draw him out of his silence, for he'd always been known for his reclusiveness, even at the evening gatherings with fellow-coun-trymen and neighbors out on the back patio. Everyone jabbered away while your father sat deep in thought, perhaps considering the great misfortune of those who cannot tolerate solitude. A mute host, ascetic even in the face of gregariousness, he would have preferred to escape to his room, to commune with the silence of white walls and, the Book in hand, to trace the depos-ing of a sultan who had ruled an Andalusian city, fol-lowing his footsteps through the seven rooms of an impenetrable castle, until reaching the last room, where the sinister destiny of the invader was sealed.

Your father usually preferred to be alone when he was reading, though occasionally he would tolerate someone approaching him when the shop was empty, his hands resting on the pages reflected in the glass showcase. Just such a discreet intruder, I pretended to be admiring some fabric he'd brought back from one of his trips to the southern coast. Anyone seeing him there behind the massive counter pouring all his concentration into the pages of a thick book might well suppose there was an abyss between him and the showcases. As there was be-tween him and anyone he didn't know: he was always silent or at best taciturn with strangers. He was more open with me, maybe because I knew Emilie and had been a friend of Emir's, or because I was willing to ob-serve his solitude from a distance.

One day I found him wandering among the showcas-es. I got the impression that something was bothering him, though he greeted me with a smile and unrolled a map of the Amazon basin. I asked, out of the blue, if he were searching for Paradise, some paradise on earth.

"That's not a question for a simple silk trader," he replied, as unruffled as ever. He walked to the counter and went on. "In this world, paradise can be found on the back of a sorrel, in the pages of a few good books, and between the breasts of a woman."

Taking advantage of his willingness to talk (he'd been known to proclaim that silence is more beautiful and meaningful than a multitude of words), I asked him to tell me a little about his past. He was quiet for a moment, his fingers tracing the almost infinite web of rivers that defies the rigor of cartographers and incites men to adventure. He drew an imaginary circle at the western margin of the map and as he spoke his narrative sounded so carefully woven it seemed meant to be written down. The obsession I cultivated in Manaus, of jotting down people's stories, filled notebook after notebook. One of these notebooks contains quite an accurate record of what your father told me that afternoon in 1929.

THE VOICE OF
THE FATHER

MY TRIP ENDED in a place it would be an exaggeration to call a city. By convention or convenience, its inhabitants insisted on considering it part of Brazil, which seems as arbitrary as the three or four countries within the Amazon region considering an imaginary line through an infinite horizon of trees a border. And here, in this misty jungle unknown even to most Brazilians, my Uncle Hanna had seen combat for the Glory of the Brazilian Republic; he even attained the rank of colonel, while back in Lebanon he had been a sheep farmer and fruit wholesaler to the cities on the southern coast. We never understood why he had gone to Brazil in the first place, but we were amazed and dismayed by his letters, which took months to arrive. They told of devastating epidemics; barbarous acts of cruelty committed with singular finesse by men who worshiped the moon, innumerable battles stained the colors of twilight, men who ate the meat of their own kind as if savoring a leg of lamb, palaces surrounded by splendid gardens and sloping walls with pointed arched windows facing the western sky where the moon of Ramadan appears. They also described the dangers to be braved— rivers so vast their surfaces were endless mirrors, reptiles with iridescent skin brilliant enough to wake him up just as his eyelids were closing at the sacred siesta hour, and a certain poison the natives made no belligerent use of but that, on penetrating the skin, would put a person to sleep and induce terrible dreams, concentrations of pure unhappiness distilled from his or her life.

Eleven years after emigrating to Brazil, probably around 1941, Uncle Hanna sent us two photographs of himself, which were each glued to pieces of cardboard and then glued back to back. The photographs came with a note that said: "There is another picture sealed between the two pieces of cardboard, but it should only be looked at when the next family member arrives here." When my father read this, he looked at me and said: "It's your turn to cross the ocean and explore the unknown on the other side of the earth."

I knew that Manaus was the name of the place where Uncle Hanna lived, and I knew that everyone knew everyone there, that even the most ferocious enemies rubbed elbows occasionally. The journey itself turned out to be very difficult: more than three thousand miles and several weeks long. Sometimes, especially at night, it seemed as though we few adventurous folk on the ship were the only survivors of some catastrophic event. I lost all sense of time. When finally, one intensely hot night, the captain's voice announced we were about to drop anchor just outside the port of Manaus, it was hard to believe we had really arrived anywhere at all. Not a single light was to be seen on the horizon. Above our heads there was a festival of stars, the reflections of which danced on the surface of the river along an endless imaginary line beside the boat; only the darkness between the two proved there was land.

I anxiously awaited daybreak. In spite of its great mystery, nature is almost always punctual here. At five-thirty everything in the invisible world before us was absolutely still; minutes later light dawned like a sudden revelation, tinged with many shades of red like a carpet extending on the horizon, where thousands of sparkling wings appeared: flashes of ruby and pearl. During this brief interval of tenuous luminosity, I noticed an immense tree, roots and crown stretching in opposite directions toward clouds and water, and I felt comforted, imagining that it was the tree of the seventh heaven.

With everyone around me asleep, I witnessed that sunrise alone. It was the most intense I have ever experienced. In time I came to understand that a vision of a singular landscape can change a man's destiny, making him less of a stranger to the land he's about to walk upon for the first time.

Before six o'clock, everything was visible: the sun looked like a single, brilliant eye lost in the blue roof of heaven and, out of what had been a dark stain spreading before the boat, the city was born. It wasn't much bigger than many villages huddled between the mountains of my country, but the fact that the land was flat accentuated the repetition of wooden hut after wooden hut and exaggerated the splendor of the larger stone structures: the church, the military garrison, one or two large private homes in the distance. Needless to say, there were no palaces; those had been inventions of Hanna, the most imaginative of my father's brothers. Back home in our village, a huge leg of lamb served as the stimulus to get him telling a world of stories; the older folks would listen raptly and the blind and deaf patriarch of Tarazubna would interrupt, adding a word or gesture during moments of hesitation, when something was left out.

I stepped off the boat onto a narrow plank and walked through a crowd of people eagerly awaiting news, relatives, or packages. They all seemed to be barefoot, openmouthed, and a little sad. Some looked just plain hungry and there was no hiding it. I searched the crowd for Uncle Hanna, but no one looked anything like him. Finally a tall, beefy young man slouching against a red wall caught my eye. Somehow I found the words in Portuguese to ask him if he happened to know the man in the two-sided picture I held in my hand.

"That's my father," he said solemnly, staring me in the eye and ignoring the photos. I embraced him and asked after Hanna; he merely pointed toward the horizon, where the sunrise was still blazing, and began walking down the only street in the village. Clearly I would be wise to follow. Little by little I realized that the wooden houses lining both sides of the street looked completely deserted; I concluded that their inhabitants were all milling around down at the dock. As I padded along the soft earth after the man who claimed to be Hanna's son, I saw that it must have rained before daybreak (perhaps while I was praying), because not only was the ground soggy but the laundry and foliage were dripping wet. Three hundred yards or so later, the street (and the village) ended. We crossed a rickety wooden bridge over the igarapé that separated town from forest.

It had never occurred to me that Hanna might live in the jungle, like an ascetic in the thousand-year-old cedar forests of Lebanon! But it stands to reason that solitude means different things in different places. An almost nocturnal darkness reigned here, and the air was thick on the narrow, tortuous path beneath the trees. I began to have my doubts about the young man who claimed to be Hanna's son and chided myself for having believed him, wondering if I were walking into an ambush. Like anyone in a potentially dangerous situation, I was scared; I considered saying something, or

turning around and walking back in the opposite direction, but as I hesitated between alternatives the terrain
suddenly changed and a beam of light revealed the end
of the path. A kind of clearing up ahead seemed a
strange interruption of this shadowy world. I don't
know why, but I began staring at first one, then the
other picture of Uncle Hanna, flipping the cardboard
over in my hand as I walked. The two images, which
before had looked identical, now looked somehow different. I imagined this was the result of some chemical
change during processing. Two prints from the same
plate probably always result in two distinct images, I
told myself. I flipped the cardboard nervously in my
hands, comparing the two portraits. The gradually im-
proving light emphasized certain slight differences: the
curve of the eyebrows, the prominence of the cheek-
bones, the texture of the hair. The figure of the young
man up ahead caught my eye. I stepped out into a flat,
treeless clearing of beaten earth, an enormous hole in
the jungle.

I didn't need to be told which grave was Uncle Hanna's: the only one without a cross and images of saints.
Suddenly I remembered the photograph hidden between the two pieces of cardboard. Ripping them apart,
I found another picture of Uncle Hanna, from long
ago, before he left Lebanon; but it could just as easily
have been his son. I didn't ask for the particulars of
Uncle Hanna's death. There was no shortage of possible explanations, after years of living in a place where
fevers proliferated as widely as knife wounds. No won-

der the cemetery was larger than the village! Neither was I interested in the identity or fate of the boy's mother; I learned later from an acquaintance that she was the best-looking woman around, and that the first words of Portuguese, besides her name, that Uncle Hanna learned were: queen, pearl, marble, star, and moon. Maybe these nouns came to represent her name, dispensing with the need for the complex verb *to fall in love*. It struck me that jealousy might have been what killed him. At any rate, the first time he met a woman the son would begin avenging his father.

I lived in town for a few years. I got to know the most remote rivers and soon learned that, in addition to knowledge of the four arithmetic operations, being a businessman required a certain malevolence, daring, and disrespect, if not disregard, for some of the teachings of the Koran.

Coming to Manaus was my last adventurous impulse. I decided to stay because from a distance the cupola of the Municipal Theater reminded me of a mosque I had never seen in person but remembered clearly from pictures in books read to me when I was a child and from the descriptions of a man I'd known who had made the pilgrimage to Mecca.

I knew I was going to marry Emilie long before Emir disappeared. There were quite a lot of Middle Easterners in Manaus, almost all living in a neighborhood near the port. We Levantines always gravitate to the banks of a river or a coastline, and anywhere we go the waters we see and touch are also those of the Mediterranean.

All the bachelors spoke of Emilie with great enthusiasm and hopefulness; the older ones recalled their youth. After all, they had many decades behind them. Emilie was an only daughter, and from all I heard about her I couldn't help falling in love.

DORNER

THAT WAS HOW your father described his arrival in Brazil when I asked him about it one afternoon. The odd thing was the way he spoke, never once looking at me but gazing the whole time at the Book open before him. He leafed through it every now and then, gently stroking the pages, and the intimacy of his hands with the sacred text seemed to enliven his voice. Other episodes in his life were witnessed by the Book as well; I remember once when he waxed eloquent, though still humble, explaining several suras: the Spider, the Winds, the Resurrection, and the Overwhelming Event. One day I found him alone in the Parisian. He was sitting behind the massive counter, and the absence of the Book seemed to me a warning against returning to past conversations.

Barely waiting for me to say hello, he asked what had happened to the pictures of Emir. I believe this question had been throbbing in his mind for a long time and I'd always tried to avoid discussing that morning of the bandstand; I suspected Emilie had asked him to get the photographs from me. (She had asked me about them herself, but I always invented an excuse or changed the subject and that's the way it was left—until the next time.) Your Uncle Emílio sent away to Trieste for the oval frame the size of a human face; the precut marble and the slightly concave glass came from Italy as well. The glass was to protect from wet weather and algae, and it was so perfectly fitted to the frame that even today there's no mold on the photograph. It does have a slightly blurry look to it, but this can be attributed to the humidity and to an occasional sigh from one who, even in death, will not passively allow himself to be observed. When finally your father broached the subject, I knew I'd have to produce the photographs: his request was pronounced like an edict and, on top of that, there was Emilie. She'd spent months harping on the same string: her brother's grave remained unfinished all because of me. I knew I'd have to give in eventually, as everyone usually did when Emilie persevered, but it had been a very long time since I'd been in the darkroom, and I didn't feel up to the task. It would have been too painful to watch Emir's face slowly emerge in the chemical bath, the orchid in the hand beside his lapel like a dark heart springing from within his body. I asked a German friend of mine to make prints, life-size, as Emilie requested. He made several copies, some with quite a lot of contrast. Emir's eyebrows looked like two black arcs, thick and continuous, and his meticulously combed hair was so black it was almost blue, but none of this could disguise the despair clearly visible in his expression and in the gray furrows lining his forehead.

I had my friend print other versions with less contrast, but there was always a telltale quality, an ineradicable mark of anguish that the photograph itself perpetuated. I imagined—in one of those moments when morbidity mediates nostalgia and the effort to reverse the irreversible—I tried to imagine Emir's expression if he were to see his own face multiplied by a series of enlargements and to guess which he would choose for Emilie. When Emilie looked at the thirteen prints, she paused over the ones in which the contours and details of her brother's face were most pronounced. Silent and serene, she became absorbed in the images, perhaps wondering, "Why this expression, this drawn face, this intense agitation that the play of light and shadow reveals?" I left her alone with the photographs, noticing that she would place her hands over Emir's eyes or cover a part of his face, as if she thought that by looking at the parts of him separately she might discover whatever it was that escaped us looking at the whole. Emilie insisted on keeping all thirteen prints. She also asked for a full-body photograph to put in the frame

from Trieste. She didn't know that I had taken a hiatus
from professional photography, only picking it up again
after a long trip into the interior. A short time later I
chucked all my darkroom equipment and supplies. Actually, I traded them for a library of rare books that had
belonged to a couple of attorneys in town. My library
grew with the books I acquired from Germans fleeing
Manaus during the war years. Those were difficult
times for the German community. Many dyed their
hair black and fled to the jungle, where they got sick
and died: the survivors returned to the city after the
war to find their neoclassical mansions sacked and destroyed, and found shelter only at religious missions or
at a few of the European consulates, When the German consular agency reopened, they ordered books
from all over the world and that's also when I was able
to get Eastern literature in readable translations. My
friendship with your father prompted me to read *A
Thousand and One Nights,* in a translation by Henning.
My slow and careful reading of that book brought us
closer: for gradually I realized there were certain allu-
sions to the book, and that some episodes of his life
were adulterated transcriptions of certain tales, as if the
voice of the narrator were echoing in my friend's words.
Early in our friendship your father was cautious and reserved, but by the time I'd read the thousandth night
he had become a prodigious talker. Sometimes a person
is unveiled in the reading of a book. But the curious
thing is that your father always allowed a note of doubt
or incredulity to creep into his tale, without ever losing

the intonation and fervor of someone speaking with conviction. Actual events in the life of Emilie's family and the city of Manaus also cropped up in the versions your father told to solitary visitors to the Parisian. What made me think of this was the striking similarities between certain incidents in other peoples' lives, which, blended with elements from the Eastern texts, he incorporated into his own life. It was as if he were inventing a dubious truth that belonged to him and to others. These coincidences took me by surprise, but in the end, time blurs the differences between real life and a book. And, besides, something that surprises one man today will one day surprise all humanity. Thinking also of the photograph of Emir, I considered the fact that an image protected by a sheet of glass could evoke not just a single death in Manaus but those in the wider world as well.

HAKIM

A FTER EMIR'S DEATH, Dorner went off traveling and was gone for years. I didn't meet him until Christmas 1935, and I've been fascinated by his albums of photographs and drawings ever since. He never tired of showing Father and us children that colossal archive of images, complete with the routes of his travels traced out patiently and diligently on tiny maps. When people praised or complimented him on the job he'd done he would humbly say: "I'm sure there are glaring errors in my catalog of adventures, but I believe every traveler who seeks the unknown must live with the blessed hypothesis of making mistakes." Years later Dorner tried, unsuccessfully, to teach the history

of philosophy in a law school, though his secret passion
was botany. I spent a lot of time at his house during my
adolescence. Dorner took boundless pleasure in showing me all the historical documents he'd accumulated
in his life. He was disappointed that I showed no enthusiasm during the German lessons he gave his coun-
trymen's children and grandchildren. Noting my lack
of interest, he quipped: "All is not lost; by the time I get
back from the two Germanys your enthusiasm will have
doubled." When he left for Europe, around 1955, I
thought he would never come back. It turned out I was
the one to go into permanent exile. His trip coincided
with my leaving for the south. He wrote me copious
letters from Leipzig and Cologne; I still reread them
quite often. Every time I do I'm surprised by some subtle remark or disclosure about his time in Amazonas.
He scrutinized things with the keenness of a critic, intent on placing under a magnifying glass practically
everything he'd already studied with the naked eye. To
me, *Cattleya Eldorado* were simply two words that em-
bodied a certain mysterious quality; to Dorner they
meant a rare orchid that gave rise to other varieties of
wildly different colors like *Splendens, Ornata, Crocata,*
and *Glebelands.* On mentioning these Cattleya orchids,
he specified the size of sepals and petals, and guided
me through an eccentric nomenclature citing claviform
bulbs, leathery leaves, and aromatic flowers whose colors ranged from pale pink to deep magenta. He referred
to other Cattleyas as well, such as *Schilleriana* and
Odoratissima, and every time we visited his own person-

al orchid garden, shaded by a trellis of araroba, he would point out a wooden sign that read: AT WHAT MO-MENT DID GOD CREATE ORCHIDS?

Then there were Dorner's exhaustive forays into the jungle, where he'd stay for weeks or months and return to insist that Manaus was an urban perversion. "City and jungle are two different scenarios, two lies separat-ed by a river," he liked to say. To me, born and raised here, nature had always seemed hostile and impenetra-ble. Attempting to compensate for this powerlessness in the face of nature, I'd sit and contemplate the jungle for hours on end, in hopes that in the act of looking it-self I might decipher enigmas, or that, without my passing through the green wall, nature would somehow reveal herself more indulgent, like a perpetual and un-reachable mirage. More than the river, an inertia com-ing from who knows where paralyzed me when I thought about the crossing, the other side. Dorner struggled to accept my fear of the jungle, observing that anyone who lived in Manaus and felt no connec-tion to the river and the rain forest was a guest in a sin-gular prison: open, but only onto itself. "The act of leaving this city," Dorner would say, "implies leaving not just a space but, more importantly, a time. Do you have any idea what a privilege it is for someone, on leaving his home port, to be able to enter another time?"

When people asked Dorner if he had really quit be-ing a professional photographer, he'd say: "I've merely changed the path of my looking. I used to fix my eye on a fragment of the exterior world and press a button; now, it's the mind's eye of reflection that interests me." And I know—it's common knowledge—that he was forever writing down his impressions of Amazon life. The ethics and behavior of the area's inhabitants and everything about the identity and intimacy among whites, mixed-breed river people, and Indians were among his favorite themes. Included in one of his letters from Cologne were several pages entitled "Looking and Time in Amazonas." He maintained that the slow gestures and the lost and unfocused look of people here appeal for silence and constitute ways of resisting time or, better, remaining outside time. He disputed the widespread assumption here in the north that people are alien to everything else, born slow and sad and passive; his arguments were based on his own intensive experience in the region, on "Humboldt's cosmic pilgrimage," and also on his reading of philosophers who probed what he called "the delicate territory of the Other." The letter was full of quotations and circumlocutions: a generous strategy intended to capture the attention of the recipient, whose only response was doubt and hesitations.

But neither in our conversations nor in writing did he reply to my insinuations regarding Emir's death. Maybe it was out of respect for his pact with Emilie, since a suicide can overwhelm succeeding generations of a family. I always imagined she was the one who deciphered obscure issues, and no one dared breathe a word to anyone without her approval; all of our failures and weaknesses, when they couldn't be avoided or fore-seen, were bottled up within the closed space of the Parisian, or the new house after we moved. It wasn't just love for her brother that caused Emilie to go to such great lengths to get the photographs from Dorner. Signs of Emir's strange behavior were clearly visible in the only image of his face captured the morning he died. Emilie wanted the photograph for herself in order to make sure her brother's delirious look was not seen by the eyes of the city. I still remember finding the six-by-eight negative pressed between pieces of tissue paper and slipped among the white garments carefully folded in the bottom of the trunk lined with black velvet; I don't know where she hid it after the clock came out of the closet. Just yesterday I was in Emilie's room and there, inside the wardrobe, sat the old trunk, open and empty. I have no idea when she took all the things out of there or where she put them. Maybe she sensed that she was about to die, and got rid of everything so as to leave no clues.

I deduced from the letters from V.B. that Emir had been peevish toward Emilie ever since he'd had to threaten suicide to get her to leave the convent, and the rough draft of a letter she never sent provided some clarification of their falling out and perhaps even of her brother's tragic fate.

During the trip from Beirut to Brazil, the ship made a stop in Marseilles. One part of the letter, which I translated as best I could and which I'll never forget, went like this: "A port is a dangerous place for the young, because they almost always fall victim to a fatal virus: love." The letter is filled with expressions such as "loose woman," "indecent urges," and "temptation of the devil." Most likely, Emir wanted to remain in Marseilles or to bring someone with him to Brazil, because he was gone the entire four days they were docked there. Sick with worry, Emilie advised her other brother to alert the French police. They found Emir outside the railroad station and forcibly returned him to the ship. In one of his pants pockets they discovered, in addition to two train tickets, part of the money Emilie had packed in the trunk, buried among clothes and jewelry. When Emilie and her brothers got off the ship in Recife, their parents noticed that Emir was acting strangely; he hardly said a word to them. And at home in Manaus, over all the years the family lived there, he communicated with his sister only when their parents were present. I remember Hindié told me that during his "dizzy spells" Emir used to quote something in French. I found no reference to this phrase in the letters. The day of the funeral, I tried to get Hindié to tell me more about it, but she could barely open her eyes: there was a film of tears between her upper and lower eyelashes, and all she could get out was

"I'm all torn up, my son, reduced to rags. . . ."

The multiple copies of the picture of Emir turned out to be useful to Emilie in carrying out a vow she fulfilled religiously over a good part of her life; you must have noticed that every year, without fail, on the morning of the anniversary of Emir's death, she walked to the cathedral, knelt down facing the river, and intoned the Responses of Saint Anthony; then she'd go to the dock and ask a boatman to take her to the mouth of the Educandos igarapé, where she threw a bouquet of flowers and a picture of her brother into the river. This gesture, repeated year after year, aroused a certain curiosity in the inhabitants of the Floating City. A few of them began stopping by the house, first to ask Emilie for advice and, eventually, for alms and favors. Long before I left town (and before Emir's death, it's said) she had already taken on the responsibility of keeping washerwoman Anastácia Socorro's children fed. I tried to see this gesture as generous and spontaneous, and maybe it did contain a certain amount of spontaneity, but as for generosity . . . It must be said that the maids and washerwomen at the house didn't receive a penny for their work, which was a common enough practice here in the north. But generosity is revealed or disguised in the way we treat the Other, in our acceptance or rejection of the Other. Emilie was always grumbling that Anastácia "ate like a tapir" and tried her patience by arriving on weekends accompanied by an entourage of nieces and nephews. To the bigger ones, five or six and up, Emilie assigned a job: wash the windows, dust the lamps and shutters, feed the animals, sheer or brush the sheep, and pick up the fallen leaves all over the yard. I watched in silence, painfully, guiltily, noticing as well that the servants didn't eat the same food we did, and that they skulked in their quarters next to the chicken coop during our mealtimes. There was humiliation even in the way they raised the tin spoons to their mouths. In addition, whenever possible, my brothers mistreated the maids, who sometimes didn't even last a day with all the physical and emotional violence. The only one who endured was Anastácia Socorro, because she could take anything—and because she was not very attractive physically. I can't count the times I saw her bombarded with abuse and insults just for muttering something like how she was running out of patience with having to make breakfast every time someone else would wake up, all the way through to noon. Harsh voices, curses, and blows were also part of the cruel drama that went on at the house. I remember one scene that really upset me and that, in fact, hastened my decision to leave and venerate Emilie from afar.

I was reading in my room when I heard a commotion on the stairs: shouting, wailing, a big ruckus. I ran to see what was going on and found one of my brothers dragging one of our ex-maids, with a baby in her arms, down the stairs and out the door. Emilie appeared out of nowhere, pulled them apart and tried to calm them down. Eventually, she escorted the girl to the gate and whispered something in her ear. The girl walked straight to the Parisian and told Father her story. It was one of the few times I ever saw him blind with hatred, his eyes flaming with fury. I was standing beside the kitchen window, my attention divided between the pictures in a travel book and a canopy of gray leaves rustling in the garden when his tall, slightly stooped frame appeared in the doorway. I practically snapped to attention. His leather belt was coiled around his wrist like a thin, black snake, and the sound of his feet on the stairs were unmistakable: he took huge strides, landing hard on each step. As he bounded upstairs his left hand scraped the handrail, the friction of skin on wood making a kind of intermittent screeching noise. Terrified, I could hear the scurrying, every-man-for-himself feet upstairs, and then Father, between kicks and blows on the door, using Portuguese for the first time in a fit of wrath, yelling, "No son of mine is going to spurt like an animal inside a woman's body." Then he flew downstairs in search of Emilie. The book trembled in my hands, and the pen-and-ink drawing became just a shapeless network of fine scribblings; I looked out at the yard, searching for Sálua, but couldn't find her. I didn't even have the energy to get away; I was feeling all alone and filled with torpor in the face of an angry father. The war of words with Emilie was tempestuous and brief. Father pointed out that this wasn't the first girl to show up at the Parisian, a baby in her arms, claiming, "This is your grandson, son of your son"; he insisted that he hadn't come all the way across the ocean to nourish the fruit of the random pleasures of parasites; that his sons clearly confused sex with instinct and, much more serious, had forgotten the name of God.

"God?" spluttered Emilie. "Do you think those half-breeds look to the sky and think of God? They're just a bunch of flirting tramps from the jungle that fool around with anyone who comes along and then come here begging milk and spare change."

Father cut the discussion short and walked away looking grave, more disappointed with Emilie than with my brothers. It was useless to condemn or reprimand them. Emilie always took their side; they were pearls afloat between heaven and earth, ever gleaming and visible to her eyes, and within her reach. Emilie's collusion with my brothers revolted me, and caused me to distance myself from her sometimes, even though I knew I, too, was idolized. I withdrew because I wasn't a hellion, because I was neither victim nor aggressor, because I resisted rudeness and brutality in the treatment of others. Deep inside, I believe I left the family and Manaus because I couldn't bear the brutish familiarity people assumed with their servants. I remember Dorner once said that here in the north privilege didn't derive only from wealth.

"A strange kind of slavery prevails here," he said. "Humiliation and threats are the lash; food and the illusion of integration into the boss's family are the chains and iron collar."

There was some truth in what he said. I noticed the effort Emilie put into maintaining the flame of cordial relations with Anastácia Socorro. Sometimes the two would sit together in the living room embroidering or sewing, and talking about distant times and places. These conversations always caught my attention; I'd sit nearby for hours, captivated by the narghile—the gold design on its glass base, the crimson beads forming whorls and corkscrews half-submerged in the bright pearly liquid, and the wood mouthpiece that ended in a delicate opening, like lips puckered for a kiss. Lovingly admiring that object dormant during the day, I'd listen to their voices rising and falling, as they discussed the diverse topics that brought them closer together. Anastácia was really taken with the grapevine on the small patio, its roof of leaves sprouting clusters of tiny grapes, almost white and transparent, which never grew any bigger; she made a face when she tasted them, they were so sour, not understanding the origin of the enormous bunches of full-bodied muscatel grapes that were taking over the refrigerator—that orchard of delicacies—not to mention the apples, pears, and figs that Father would bring home from the south, along with boxes of locoum with almonds, little sacks of musk, cans of dates, and tins of "tombac," the Persian tobacco for the narghile. The servants were forbidden to eat these special fruits and delicacies. Whenever I was around to witness Emilie catch Anastácia hurriedly swallowing a date, pit and all, or other treats, I'd intercede and insist that I'd offered her the last date from a box I'd just polished off. Not only did this protect the guilty party from reproach, punishment, or threat, but the very thought that a son of hers would devour immense quantities of food made Emilie absolutely delirious, as if the concept of happiness were very closely related to the act of endlessly chewing and swallowing.

Anastácia's way of thanking me was to perfume my clothes; after scrubbing and rinsing them, she'd sprinkle my shirts, sheets, and socks with lavender, and when I'd stick my hands in the pockets of my pants I'd find benjamin and cinnamon. A strange blend of scents followed me through town and issued from my open wardrobe during the night, as if invisible incense burned in some dark inner recess.

Smell was something the two women talked about quite a lot. The aroma of fruits from the south vanished if they were placed near the cupuassu or cherimoya fruit. According to Emilie, capuassu and cherimoya exuded one smell during the day and another, more intense, aroma during the night. "They're fruit to satisfy the nose, not the belly," she'd say. "When I was a little girl, only figs could make me light-headed like this." The aroma of figs was the loose end of yarn for a whole skein of stories. Mother told Anastácia about the feats of the village men in the autumn twilight stirring piles of leaves that would soon be covered with snow, stirring them with bare hands, their hairy right index fingers searching for scorpions, to provoke them, unafraid of the curling tail with a stinger that went straight through the fig proffered with the left hand. She recounted strolls in the Roman ruins, describing religious temples from previous centuries, games played riding on animals, and expeditions through huge caves carved out of mountains of snow to a convent at the edge of a cliff. "But there was another path, in the open air," she would say, flushed with excitement. There were many natural stairways made of rocks shaped by snow and wind, and they almost always led to a convent or monastery. Up on the mountain, the earth, rivers, and blue sea disappeared: the landscape of the world was reduced to a forest of black cedars and the holy river born at the foot of the mountains. Then, beyond the walls circling those splendid and solemn structures, another landscape would miraculously come into view: streams winding though woods, grapevines, olive and fig trees spreading out around the cloister, the chapel, and the cells where the devotees, nourished by religion, took flight for heaven on the wings of a mountain.

Expressionless, staring fixedly without taking her eyes off Emilie's face, Anastácia would take advantage of a pause to gather herself up and ask: What does the sea look like? What's a ruin? Where's Balbek? Sometimes Emilie would wrinkle her brow and nudge me, I would answer Anastácia's questions. It was curious sometimes how whole sentences came out of your grandmother's mouth in Arabic without her realizing it; probably at those moments she was far away, far from me, from Anastácia, the house, and Manaus. I'd stop contemplating the arabesques on the pipe and wonder aloud about this or that, trying to take the conversation in a different direction, doing a turnaround in time and space, leaping from the Mediterranean to the Amazon, from snow and wind to sultry weather, from mountains to plains. Then, before Anastácia could begin her side of the conversation, Emilie would put down her needle and thread and order her to make Turkish coffee and serve it in the Chinese porcelain cups, which were so small that the first sip seemed like the last. Something vague or mysterious about Anastácia's way of talking had a hypnotic effect on my mother. Unlike Father and Dorner and many of our neighbors, Emilie had never lived in the interior of Amazonas. Like me, she had never crossed the river. Emilie's visible world consisted of Manaus alone. Her other world throbbed in memory. Spellbound by Anastácia's melodious voice, Emilie marveled at her descriptions of the climbing plant that was said to drive away envy, the mottled leaves of a caladium that multiplied a man's fortune, the preparations of native healers who recognized in certain jungle grasses the antidote to relieve thirty-six pains of the human body. "Then there are the herbs that don't cure anything but stir up a person's mind. All it takes is one sip of steaming liquid for a Christian to dream many different lives in a single night."

Other people might have considered these revelations of dubious veracity, but not Emilie. You'll still find caladium and climbing vines in the garden, interspersed with ornamental plants. Emilie set out the seedlings and, under Anastácia's direction, every seven days for seven months applied a homemade fertilizer mix of chicken manure and powdered charcoal. The result was the thick wall of mossy green that surrounds the fountain, and the thicket of caladium beside the chicken coop. I remember snakes used to make their nests there and killed quite a few chickens over the years. That didn't bother Emilie. "I'd rather live with snakes than with envy," she used to say.

Anastácia would talk for hours on end, using her fingers, her hands, her whole body to imitate the way an animal moved, the sudden leap of a cat, the way a fish would dart into the air after a bug, the precarious flight of a young bird. When I think back on that maelstrom of words populating whole afternoons, I realize that in using her voice to conjure experience and imagination, Anastácia was really buying a rest from her labors, a lull in her arduous workday. The whole time she was telling stories, real life stopped and took a deep breath. And Anastácia's voice planted inside the house—inside me and Emilie—visions of a mysterious world: not exactly the world of the jungle, but that of the imaginary world of a woman who talked in order to rest, who invented in order to avoid physical labor, as if speech alone permitted the momentary suspension of her martyrdom. Emilie just let her talk, though once in a while her puzzled expression would ask the meaning of an indigenous word or a phrase not used in the city, something pertaining to the life of a washerwoman, to a long-ago time, to a forgotten place beside a river, things outside our experience. During these moments of incomprehension, Emilie's perplexed face would turn to me also, but I was powerless to help. The three of us would just sit there, resigned to the weight of a silence Emilie attributed to "the tricks of the Brazilian language." That silence hinted at so many things, and made us so uncomfortable. . . . It was as if we had to stop talking in order for something to be revealed. These may have seemed to Emilie moments of impasse, moments of acute impatience at an unresolved question. But it was

Anastácia who always broke the silence, usually with a single word. First, she'd simply pronounce the name of a bird, a bird until then mysterious and unseen, and then off she'd go describing it in detail: red primary feathers, blue-black body, and half-open beak emitting a song she would imitate as few with the skill to imitate nature's melodies can. The description had the effect of opening a dictionary to a luminous page, one glance at which made clear the word in question, and with sense came form, the bird emerging from the dark crown of a tree and slowly taking shape before our eyes.

IT'S A SHAME you never met Anastácia's uncle, Lobato Naturidade. He was the one who found and retrieved Emir's body and became a friend of the family, and a friend of Dorner, who dubbed him "The Prince of White Magic." Lobato was short, thick, and the color of putty. He was renowned for his strength; at age eighty he could still row all day long against the current. I've never met a less talkative man, but you could read on his face all the answers to the questions he was asked. None of us knew much about him, and Anastácia Socorro clammed up whenever anyone asked. I don't have any idea how, but somehow Dorner discovered that Lobato could speak fluent Nhengatu and years before had been a famous storyteller, the kind that inspires rapt silence as soon as he opens his mouth. When he first came to Manaus he was known as Tacumá—his real name—and he was famous as a clairvoyant. People sought him out whenever a child straggled off from her parents and got lost in the twisting, turning alleys of the poorest neighborhoods, which were often flooded by the water of the igarapés. Inhabitants of nearby villages and towns came to him for help in finding people lost in the web of rivers and jungle. No one ever discovered what method he used to find them. All we knew was that he would stay up all night and at dawn would point with both arms in a certain direction and that's where the missing person would be found. Dorner also learned that he had lived in Cayenne for a while with a rich Creole, and that he had almost gone with her when she decided to move to Paris.

Dorner had a way about him: he could get a stone to talk if he put his mind to it. I confess that I personally never heard Lobato utter a single word; when he looked at you, though, even for less time than a handshake, his look unquestionably created a closer connection than the meeting of fingers. Emilie treated him with a respect that bordered on veneration. His visits to the house were rare, but the minute he appeared on the doorstep, a worn, drab leather sack of herbs and medicinal plants on his back, the whole neighborhood knew that someone in the family was ailing. He was a master in the art of treating rheumatism, swelling, colds, stomach pains, and a range of other common illnesses; he'd make a tonic of herbs mixed with honey and olive oil, and massage the sore or swollen area with a paste consisting of the crushed bark of several different trees, a few drops of tincture of arnica, and a pinch of Dutch salve. Dorner eventually revealed the ingredients and exact proportions, at the request of Dr. Hector Dorado. I remember when Dr. Dorado came back from Europe and humbly announced: "I had to go all the way to London to be convinced that successful treatment for many ailments here can be ascribed to the jungle dwellers' profound understanding of local plants." Dorner and I were close friends of Hector's, and we'd imagined that the idea of a native healer ministering to people in their hour of suffering might wound the pride of a graduate of the University of Bahia medical school with a graduate degree from the London School of Tropical Medicine. To our surprise, our doctor friend had it in mind to meet Lobato even before he began complaining of the heat and the extreme difference between London and Manaus. At first, the closest he managed to get was peeking through the leaves at a prolonged massage session on Emilie's rheumatic leg. Dorado had the patience of Job; he stood and watched the whole thing, from the preparation of the balm through to the end. In this way, from a distance, he gradually became familiar with the fumigations and learned the properties of mallows, crajiru, and certain varieties of poppy and roots from the jungle. A few weeks later, he wasn't surprised in the least to learn that inhaling the steam from a gourdful of a certain scalding-hot liquid that "reeked to high heaven" enabled a mere mortal to experience the sensation of the infinite. Dorner listened silently to his friend's discoveries and passionate convictions. Later, he confided to me, not without an ironic smile, that the locals were often rather slow to notice certain evidence.

There were some who favored Emilie's friendship with Lobato and others who rejected it out of hand. You must remember the Commander's son-in-law, Américo, the way he suffered. He'd been having daily insulin injections since the day he took his first steps. Emilie couldn't accept that "barbarous" therapy forever and advised Esmeralda to ask Lobato to have a look at him, which she did, and the local doctors took great offense. Dr. Rayol blamed Emilie. "It's just like a nomad immigrant to rely on the quackery of a witch doctor like that," he proclaimed to his patients. "If this kind of thing spreads, before long people will believe fiddlewood tea can cure cancer." The man did have a point, since Shalom Benemou's wife, another neighbor and friend of the family, did ask Lobato to treat that very illness, but the Indian knew his limitations. As for Américo's problem, though, the cure was like one of those stories in the Scriptures: after a few months of treatment, he felt well enough to give up his injections forever.

"I no longer wake up feeling as if my days are numbered!" he announced. And I remember he became so enthusiastic about life that he dug his Spanish violin out of the cellar; after that, the late-night hours became even more deeply silent with Paganini solos, as if he were playing to glorify the silence. In any case, Américo survived for many years under Lobato's care.

Some said the treatment consisted of an alcoholic extract from paricá-rana and sapupira seeds; Emilie swore that it also included a brew prepared from leaves and shavings from the roots and stems of jacareúba, cherimoya, and papaw. Lobato never confirmed or denied any of it. And, to everyone's surprise, he refused the lifetime salary Américo's family offered him, accepting instead an image of Saint Joaquim, from Alcobaça.

The defamatory stories about Lobato spread by doctors and patients were very distressing to Emilie. He was said to have poisoned one poor soul and blinded several others by pouring a red palm extract into their inflamed eyes; there were reports of diabolical rituals to summon the spirit of Evil and penetrate the entrails of the victim. And there was no shortage of people ready to revile the methods he supposedly used to induce abortions and cure venereal diseases: fetid brews, indecent massages of the belly and other curvaceous parts of the body. Rumor had it that the women became sterile and the men impotent. It was Lobato's nomadic life, however, the fact that he had no fixed home, that seemed to bother people most. He was reportedly seen entering the carcass of an abandoned boat, surrounded by vultures, half-buried in a sea of garbage, at the edge of an igarapé. There were those who swore he frequented squalid huts, their walls covered with images of strange saints that looked either drunk or crazy. Somewhere near each tumbledown shack, a circle of luminous dots bloomed in the pitch of night, illuminating bottles of cachaça, dead chickens, and piles of profane medallions. The nasty rumors swirling around that peaceable, practically invisible man constituted an attack on an entire tradition, one that was very much alive in Manaus, pulsing in the heart of the outlying neighborhoods behind the doors of precarious, rain-drenched houses.

But more astonishing than all the slander leveled against Lobato was the news that he and Anastácia Socorro were related. For years we'd assumed that she knew the Prince of White Magic only from his visits to the house, but in fact it was he who had suggested that she come to us looking for work in the first place; somehow he knew that Emilie needed a woman to do the laundry and that she would take to his niece. Anastácia and Lobato never exchanged more than a glance in our presence, and we imagined their common interest in medicinal plants was merely a coincidence. Much to the rest of the family's surprise, the revelation that the two were related altered the relationship between the two women; Anastácia was more familiar with visitors and gained Emilie's protection; her load of domestic tasks was reduced and the number of lazy afternoons multiplied. No longer treated as a household slave, Anastácia began living the life of a respected employee. The sudden upgrading of her privileges was to be ephemeral, however. In spite of Emilie's stern expressions of disapproval, my brothers were guilty of frequent lapses; they simply could not accept the idea of an Indian woman sitting at the dining-room table with the family, touching her lips to

the same cutlery and crystal and china cups as the rest
of the family. A kind of disgust and revulsion was
written on their faces; they stopped eating with their
usual gusto and not a word of praise was heard for the
lamb pastries, date squares with cream, or golden rice
with almonds exuding an aroma of toasted onions.
Sitting there silently, her face harrowed with wrinkles,
that woman seemed to sap the food of its flavor and
aroma and to squelch both voices and gestures, as if
her silence or her mere presence, which was silence in-
carnate, was an obstacle to the regular life of the family. Without anyone's saying a word about it, Anastácia
withdrew from the intimacy that had prompted my
brothers' disgust, Emilie's distress, and general tension at mealtimes, one of the rare moments when the
family customarily hoisted the ceasefire flag. Emilie's
cooking had always been a unifying force, and the
news of the day (a robbery, someone arriving in town
or leaving, a wedding, someone being widowed) provided a context within which to declare a truce and
forget our rancor. I used to watch my father out of the
corner of my eye, and sometimes, without actually seeing it, I could tell that his wandering gaze had fallen
on the face of the woman singled out and judged by
the others. I always imagined my father alone with
God. Dorner disagreed: "That's an exaggeration; we're
never alone with God." He informed me that the Benemou family read the Talmud together, in groups of
two or three. I told him that, for my father, when it
came to reading the suras there was no such thing as

kindred eyes, because only the Book shared his solidarity: the words were engraved on his solitude.

And so our relationship with the washerwoman Anastácia became less clearly defined, more amorphous. At a distance from the table she was less of an intimate and less of an intruder. Appetites returned, voices were once more raised in praise of Emilie's divine touch in the kitchen, and discussions of the day's events were resumed. There was the Sunday afternoon duel between two men on a deserted street, for example, a confrontation the entire city had anxiously anticipated, concerned that, whichever of the two died, his death should not become just an anecdote but a lasting event that touched all our lives. Actually, death passed unnoticed in Manaus only when it lacked agony and cruelty; otherwise it took on a memorable character, impressed on time and resistant to forgetfulness, as if the tragic loss of one individual did in fact implicate one and all. This was certainly the case with the duel between Kasen and Anuar Nonato: they died in each other's arms in front of the cathedral, like long-lost brothers finding each other at last at the moment of death. Another memorable death was when Selmo was hanged from the tallest, leafiest tree on the Flores highway and then drawn and quartered by all the people who hated him—and there were many.

If nothing horrific happened in a given year, folks appealed to memory: stories were retold with new details, victims relived their agony in voices that stridently disputed others' memories of the event. Life was not terribly peaceful. You witnessed what happened to Soraya Ângela and observed again and again Emilie's obvious (though sometimes furtive) torment whenever she was reminded of her brother's death. As time passed it seemed that she grew more attached to Emir and less reconciled to his disappearance. Twenty-some years after that morning at the bandstand, Emilie remained utterly devoted to a particular philanthropic practice to which my father raised no objections, at first. After all, didn't the Koran suggest the exact same thing in one of the suras?

I don't know how long after I left Manaus she continued this annual event, but the whole time I lived there Emilie dedicated an entire day to making sure the inhabitants of the Floating City were provided for. The previous night, the house always took on a party atmosphere. It's odd to think of setting apart a day to commemorate all the days leading up to someone's death. Emilie would rise early and hang glass vials of nectar for the hummingbirds on the branches of the jambo trees. They looked like crystal birds sucking on the breast of nature, drinking yellow liquid the color of dawn. The flowerpots and window boxes were watered and the porcelain vases filled with begonias and tulips from our French neighbors' flower gardens. Everything looked so much more cared for than it does now: the stone fountain throbbing white, the mirrors so spotless they reflected more than just an echo of our gestures. Everyone from the maids and their children to Emilie's protégés joined in the housecleaning. Hindié, Mentaha, and Yasmine helped prepare the refreshments, a culinary grab bag of Middle Eastern and Amazonian dishes. The sweets were carefully arranged in straw baskets so numerous that they covered the stone floor in the pantry and kitchen; even the corridors were impassable. At day's end, Emilie inspected the whole house and gave last-minute instructions to the boys, because there were always a few more spiderwebs and termite nests in the corners of the uninhabited rooms, stains on the floorboards, and mildew on some of the inside walls. When finally she said goodnight and went off to say her prayers and go to bed, she looked so tired she seemed to have aged, as if the entire day's accumulation of seconds were pulsing in every molecule of her body. But the next morning Emilie was luminous. She wore a black suit and a single string of pearls outlining the plunging neckline. Her marble-smooth face was framed by wavy hair, and from behind her ear a jambo flower blossomed, the same intense red as her lips. When she appeared at the top of the stairs, Father shivered and bit his lip, hurt or jealous, perhaps, certainly agitated and fascinated by that morning vision, the purest version of beauty. Not that he was surprised to see her dressed up like that; it was, after all, the anniversary of a death. But the fact is that on that particular day of the year, the black she wore was more than mourning, it was magnificence. She adopted a willowy stance, wore her sapphire ring on her left hand, and, to everyone's surprise, put on mascara. Her nails shone with clear polish, and she carried a black brocade purse, a vase of flowers, and the picture of Emir.

By the time Emilie arrived home at midday from her trip to the church and the river, a line of people waiting in the scalding sun stretched almost all the way from the door to the bandstand. Each year the line swelled with more urchins and beggars and sick people, who displayed their sores and decaying limbs and were directed to Hector Dorado. Many of the grateful brought gifts, which they preferred to call "little keepsakes for the mother of us all." These included objects, animals, and plants from the four corners of Amazonia: birds and reptiles, both live and stuffed, a precious nightingale from the river Negro, cuttings of vines, ferns, and palms, phosphorescent fish, embalmed piranhas, and even a perfect replica of a sacred oar inscribed with the story of an indigenous tribe. Emilie hung the oar on the living-room wall next to a piece of cedar from Lebanon. Both are gone now, who knows where or how. That back room near the servants' quarters, where you and your brother used to play hide-and-seek, was constructed just to store all the gifts accumulated over the years. Dozens of the fish still swim in the pool beside the fountain, and I was amazed to see that the alligators had grown so large there's now a wire enclosure for them, which was never there before. The gigantic bird cage, that transparent, sonorous construction, is new, too, because Emilie always used to make a point of having only wooden cages.

It would never have crossed Emilie's mind to give any of those lively creatures away. In fact, when a couple of charitable organizations working in the poorest neighborhoods insistently requested that she raffle off some of her "keepsakes" so the money could be used for clothing, food, and medication for the poor, she smiled and shook her head. "These things are like relics to me," she told the nuns from Saint Vincent de Paul's, sounding almost apologetic. No one dared contradict her, especially once she began to inventory each item received.

One of Anastácia Socorro's protégés was designated inventory clerk. On the morning of the offerings he stood beside Emilie as each person in line kissed her left hand and was given some food. Expedito Socorro recorded the name of the person and the origin of his or her gift on a small piece of paper; the paper was attached to the object, and over the months Expedito busied himself gluing labels and classifying the keepsakes, separating them into animal families and even indicating the type of wood (a manta ray made of andira wood, a toucan of brazilwood, a tapir of ita-uba) and the kinds of feathers and fruit seeds used for the bracelets and necklaces. It's no wonder Expedito ended up working in the letter-sorting department of the post office, since his years of experience recording and classifying had given him impressive paper-handling and sorting skills. In order to stay on good terms with the religious charities, Emilie gave them the mountains of fruit people brought her. As the years passed, Father began to mock this festival of benevolence, remarking: "This is some strange philanthropy! You take from the poor to give to the poor." He no longer hid his irritation on that most agitated day of the year, insisting he had to leave the house because there was too much hubbub for his afternoon nap. Perhaps, in his heart of hearts, he even wished the mystical birds of Attar's poetry would swoop down and stone that multitude of noisy Christians. Emilie's revenge for his ridicule was to visit the Parisian's storeroom and make off with remnants of cotton and chintz to donate to the nuns. I myself was an accomplice on some of these raids, which amounted to stealing what already belonged to us. Noticing my fear and dismay, Emilie justified her actions by saying she recognized the value of the store and its merchandise—after all, access to these material goods allowed her to help the needy in this world. But Emilie's day of charity, celebrated with the pomp of someone commemorating their patron saint's day, lost some of its dazzle after the tragic death of Soraya Ângela. Emilie just couldn't bear (or pretend to ignore) such a merciless trick of fate, one that would rock the faith of any believer and that revealed an inexplicable paradox: that fervent devotion could be undermined by a terrible curse, by some cruel and irreparable event such as the loss of a loved one, threatening generosity and charity that had developed over decades—it was as if the most shadowy corner of heaven were dumping on the house of the devoted an unforeseeable, absurd, but inevitable punishment, transforming a servant of the Lord into a fragile and powerless shadow persecuted by the Devil. That's why it was Emilie, and not Father, who became so dispirited and passive, especially over the last years I lived at home. She became stuck, vegetating, in a time outside time, and claimed to her friends that the day-to-day routine, as tedious as inactivity to a paraplegic or an amputee, threatened to darken life itself.

I didn't search for the causes of her despondency. That would have been a fruitless enterprise, since we were powerless in the grip of our mutual attachment, and any symptom of distress and discouragement in either of us would soon contaminate the other. Contagious anxieties, my idolatry of Emilie, her interference in my life—all of it was accentuated by the fact that I understood her when she spoke Arabic. Talking to me, my mother didn't have to translate her thoughts, or feel her way through the words, hesitate in the choice of a verb, or stumble over syntax. And I could feel how, bursting with pleasure, peerless, untouchable, she chose the paths of affection: a look, a gesture, a word. When I communicated my decision to leave Manaus in front of my siblings, she expressed her dismay with a verbal torrent that only we two understood. I realized that there was something twisted in her attitude. Defenseless, dumbfounded, perhaps hating us both, the others were excluded, banished from the patio. And I thought: this is why she didn't teach anyone Arabic but me, so that we'd be confidantes, so that we'd be alone together even at the moment of separation. And when the moment came, she didn't prohibit, condemn, or accuse; she simply insisted that I feel—in all its intensity, like a bomb going off inside me—the pain of separation. Breaking the sacred habit of siesta hour, she waited for the others to go off to their rooms and, once we were alone, gave herself over entirely to the symphonic poem of farewell. Every now and then she'd fall silent, lean toward me, and lightly touch my eyes with her fingertips; she stroked my eyebrows and cheeks, closed my eyelids, grazing my eyelashes with the skin on the back of her hand; closing the five fingers of the hand that caressed me, she laid them over her heart. Then, slowly, she sat back, her eyes never leaving mine. The air was dense, a sultriness tinged with musk. I breathed deeply and, almost swooning, surrendered to the painful sensation of anticipated longing, picturing myself aboard a ship that would never return to these waters. At one point Emilie got up and went to the kitchen. When she returned, with a pitcher of juice and a tray full of pistachios, almonds, sesame cakes, and figs, we couldn't hide our embarrassment that both of us had red eyes and voices choked with emotion.

It was an afternoon of promises and secrets laced with caresses and laughter. But when we laughed, life itself seemed suspended in its course, because it was a convulsive, raw, almost baleful laughter. Emilie granted all my requests to the letter. She convinced Father that I should continue my studies at the far end of the country and that I'd need a monthly stipend that she herself determined. She never wrote me a line, but we exchanged photographs regularly, intuitively understanding this to be the only way to preserve idolatry at a distance. The last thing she said to me that afternoon (before the house was plunged into the twilight flurry of preparations and arrivals of friends and relatives for dinner and gambling around the narghile) was: "I hold your eyes here inside me." Emilie sent me photographs over almost twenty-five years, and I studied them, trying to decipher the riddles and anxieties of her life, and the metamorphosis of her body. I learned of Father's death from a photograph she sent of herself seated in the rocking chair next to the empty armchair, which was covered with a white sheet, the one he always occupied beside her on Sunday mornings and holidays. There she sat, the two gold rings gleaming on her left hand, her black eyes shining from behind the net veil that hid half her face. That was the next to last time I heard from her, some eight years ago. Not long after Father's death I received the two last photographs, together in the same envelope. One of them was a close-up of her face, smooth as ever, framed by a silvery mantilla. Maybe it was the intensity of the flash or the profusion of candles flickering around her, but the mantilla and wisps of hair seemed to fall over her forehead and shoulders like phosphorescent thistle leaves. She was wearing a minimum of makeup, and her expression bespoke both unyielding serenity and the imperious attitude of the sculpted faces of the saints set into glass-covered niches lining both sides of the church, with its doors flung open to the port, lit by the morning sun. My mother's face, the saints' faces, the candles, the flames, and the niches—an amazing perfection of details. The photograph was dated the fifth of June and was the only color picture she ever sent me; the frame was made of marbleized Schoeller paper, and the lower right-hand corner of the picture bore the imprint of the Kahn brothers' photographic laboratory.

The other picture was totally different: Emilie posing in the middle of the patio surrounded by a Garden of Delights. Almost everything in that image brought me back to the distant afternoon I had announced my decision to leave Manaus. She was wearing the same silk dress with black hand-embroidered flowers, which suited her still-slender body as well as the state of mourning imposed by the recent death of her husband. She was sitting just where we sat, in the same wicker chair alongside an identical empty one where I had leaned back into the smell of musk. I contemplated that photograph as one contemplates the album of a life consisting of transparent pages woven in a dream. As I studied it, there was no way not to hear Emilie's voice, to see her body materialize on the patio in front of the fountain, where threads of crystalline water spurted from the mouths of the four stone angels like the liquid corners of an invisible, hollow, airborne pyramid. If I'd never seen that photograph, I would have been able to consider all the others separately, or to close my eyes to all the pictures sent to me over the long years, or simply to capture something fleeting from those images, something that escapes reality and contests a truth, refutes the evidence. Because the thing that most struck me in the photo was the revelation of a real moment and a palpable situation. I felt as if I were there beside

Emilie in the other wicker chair, attentive to her expression and to her voice, which undertook no interrogation—in fact seemed not even to resist my leaving forever. The voice and image brought back a world of disillusion, where a downcast face behind a thick veil heralds a death that was already under way. Emilie talked in order to remove this veil woven so long ago, which little by little was threatening to cover her whole life. And the face in the photograph seemed to lay bare all the disappointments, the false steps, and the suffering since the very moment Emilie noticed the prominence of her daughter's belly, even before Samara Délia herself was aware of it. For three or four months Samara refused to believe in the other body expanding inside hers, until the day she could no longer leave the house, until the morning she woke up and couldn't leave her room. She remained confined, alone, for five months, all too close to that invisible someone, that still limp, doubly hidden other life. Only Emilie came to her room to visit her, as if that forbidden place were dangerous, a den of contagion, to be avoided like the plague. And on the night Soraya was born, the entire house remained isolated from the screams, from the comings and goings of Emilie's friends, who had been summoned to help her with the washbasin, cloths, and compresses, amid many praying voices. For months afterward, no one was allowed even to pass in front of the door to her room, and as life grew in secret, furtively, the small, doleful world of seclusion was rigidly maintained: a dark, shadowy aquarium in the middle of the

house, where not a clatter or a moan, not a single extravagance of sound betrayed the presence of the two
bodies, as if mother and daughter had renounced
everything as they waited for absolution and acknowl-
edgment.

Emilie was the only person who consented to their
survival. It took almost a year for Samara's brothers to
accept their hidden presence; sometimes we completely
forgot that those two alien beings even existed. Our
distance, and their invisibility, became a habit; behind
the closed door to Samara Délia's room there might
just as well have been heaps of rubble or household objects that had fallen into disuse. But Emilie knew that
one day, by force of habit, we would move from insis-
tence on living with something hidden toward a new
tolerance. And then one morning, I remember I was
the first to see the child crawling around on the patio,
pale and confused, exploring her new space, wondering
at the landscape, the angles and shape of the fountain,
and totally stupefied by the animals. And you. She
stopped in front of you, touched your face and hair,
and looked at Emilie and Samara Délia as if to ask
where you had come from. You were four years old and
must have wondered the same thing. A few days later,
you went up to Samara Délia and asked where she'd
been for so long, and if she had any news from that
woman who lived far away and only came to visit you
once in a blue moon. Embarrassed, Samara searched
for an answer or excuse, but before she could think of
anything to say Emilie took you on her lap and whis-

pered something in your ear; you looked at Soraya with curiosity, smiled, and as soon as Emilie put you down you ran over and took Soraya's hand. I remember the two of you heading off to see the animals, the waterspouts, the shell-work mosaics in the fountain, and the hotbed, before disappearing into the white caladium and maidenhair ferns. You two used to get lost in there every morning, ensconced until noon, when my brothers woke up and Emilie came looking for you to take Soraya Ângela to the room where my sister was waiting for her. Only two years later, when your mother came to Manaus with a baby in her arms for Emilie to care for, did you understand. Before that you must have suspected something, because Soraya never joined in your simple word games; in your short conversations, you were the only participant; you'd cry, thinking she didn't like you, or that her muteness was some kind of magic to paralyze you, to put a spell on you, like someone faced with something she's never seen and who's afraid of the surprise about to be revealed. But it was neither dislike nor a spell, and you were the first to know. You asked all the grown-ups, "How come she never says anything? Why doesn't she answer when I talk to her?" It seemed absurd to my sister that a child would notice and remark on something she herself was still struggling to accept. Because the tone of your questions inferred fact, and as Soraya's mother she'd been feeling that the secret of an "irregularity," a "birth defect" of some kind, was no longer something she could hide. From then on she restricted her daughter to their bedroom and the back area of the house and forbade any contact with other children or with visitors.

For the first two years no one but Samara and Emilie was allowed to touch Soraya. I remember once as I approached her a sudden, almost inadvertent, shout made me freeze in my steps. It wasn't a shout of warning, or prohibition, or hostility; it sounded more like a venting of frustration, the kind that tears at you, a blurt of shame. As I drew back from Soraya, I noticed she didn't take her eyes off me, perhaps confused by my retreat, my cowardice in not touching her cheek as it had seemed I would. Those enormous, close-set black eyes, which dwarfed her small face, begged for contact, begged to reach out to the other, to widen her experience of the world. The look in her eyes said she was weary of a body brutalized by repetition, by the closed circle of monotony: the closed bedroom, the two women, the back confines of the house, the two other children. All she had was her eyes and the still-timid movements of her body; that gaze was an attempt to counteract the monotony, to resist life being interrupted at midday, when Emilie brought her upstairs to her mother and she was enveloped in premature night just as afternoon was beginning, her eyes buried between four walls. I watched her sometimes, from a distance, alone on the patio. Stretched out on the rust-colored tiles, she'd stare intently at one of the stone angels, unaware of anything else around her. Her gaze lingered on one of the open hands of the carefully sculpted body, which leaned forward slightly, balanced on tiptoe. Of the four identical figures, she had chosen just one, and her fascination focused on a single extremity of the saffron-tinged body, on the fingers of a hand spread open halfway between her head and the angel's. Ever since she was able to stand upright, her head had been grazing that hand: the stone fingers at child's eye level, right up against the hypnotized look of that tiny body planted alone on the red square of patio. All alone, but not abandoned, she mirrored the stillness of the stone, perhaps searching the anonymity of the sculpted material for a name; not a dead name but, rather, a lost or forgotten one, a name engraved in some corner of the statue. An entire morning would melt away in this tenuous contact: the meeting of eyes and hand. I observed both bodies, unable to reach out to them, because Soraya's mother was always watching from somewhere on the patio, attentive right up to the moment of separation. Once Soraya's gaze was jolted from the hand, she hung, limp, in her mother's arms, without kicking or in any way resisting the sudden movement that tore her from her voiceless dialogue.

The scene was repeated many times. I watched the two inseparable figures, asking myself why she had chosen that statue among the four, oblivious to everything around her (garden, animals, gushing water, family members), as their parallel shadows imperceptibly shortened to a smudge smaller than a doll's hand and then disappeared altogether. Almost without realizing it, like the child attracted by the angel's hand, or the hand magnetized by the gaze of the child, I was drawn into this game of presences and absences between mother and daughter. I spent many mornings watching the pantomime on the patio, and I even took a picture of Soraya Ângela, just once, from a distance.

There were also times when I stayed awake, keeping vigil in the night, hoping to discover I don't know what. I'd noticed that Samara Délia was never around on Wednesday and Saturday nights; she would disappear from her room, from the house, like someone in hiding, and only return home very late. Deep in the pitch of night I'd hear footsteps and the metallic sound of a key unlocking her bedroom door. She took great care that her footsteps and the turning of the key in the lock were almost soundless; but my room was right beside hers, and I was able to just barely catch or intuit the sound or its echo. I imagined her tiptoeing from one side of the room to the other, pausing between the bed and the window, kneeling in front of her daughter; I imagined all kinds of situations so as not to hear, so as to avoid listening. Because crying is infectious. The sound of crying always penetrates the wall: a fragile sheath, vulnerable to the pain of despair. After that, I understood why Samara's face looked older on Thursday and Sunday mornings, as if the previous night's sleep amounted to a confrontation with impossibility, with an insoluble or tragic situation. I thought of her sobbing and imagined she allowed herself to surrender like this in her bedroom in the dark of night because, for her daughter, the pain of despair was merely visible—a contorted, convulsed look, eyes wide or sunk deeply into her face, hands entangled in her hair, or else weeping nakedly, so as not to alter the contours of her face, and so that Soraya Ângela might remain lost in sleep, dragged along by a bit of death, victim of the silence of the nights and days. I found out later that my sister's nocturnal excursions ended at the church and that Emilie had persuaded her to be pious and chaste for the rest of her life.

"It's the only way to escape the guilt that could gnaw at you from head to toe," Emilie insisted.

At some point my sister began praying that her daughter would look like her. Samara had spent hours staring at the baby's features, ever since she was born, as if her urgent look might be capable of altering physiognomy, correcting this or that feature to make it match the beholder. There was also the pursuit of resemblance whereby two people in constant communion look more and more alike: they used to stick their faces together, like someone pressing hand to hand in prayer or meditation.

I remember the first time Samara Délia compared her daughter's hair, eyes, and lips to her own in my presence. "And if she ever learns to talk, I'm positive her voice will be exactly like mine," she added, staring pensively at the floor. It seemed to me a little early for my sister to be finding physical resemblances between her and Soraya; after all, Samara Délia's own face and body, and even her voice, were still developing and changing. She was a child herself—only fifteen or sixteen years old—when she became pregnant; she was still playing with your dolls, clambering up trees to pick fruit, playing pranks, and generally lightening the mood around the house. Everything changed after Soraya was born. Beyond adolescence being interrupted, I began to see certain of the child's traits in the mother. Samara Délia would suddenly stop in the middle of the patio and fix her gaze on something, and the meditative and enraptured expression on her face was very close to her daughter's. It was only much later that the physical resemblance became obvious, and they could each see themselves clearly in the other.

It was around this time that Samara and Soraya left the house together for the first and only time. They seemed guided by fear as they walked hand in hand, shunning other people, avoiding the faces of the few others exposing themselves to the burning early-afternoon sun. As for the neighbors who appeared at their windows, Samara Délia shielded herself from their looks by holding a little red umbrella in front of her face. Once in a while she'd tilt her head down toward her daughter and move her lips, pretending to talk, but words could only reach Soraya through dreams or nightmares. They walked as if glued together, Samara slowing or shortening her steps sometimes to allow Soraya to keep up. I watched from the terrace as they seemed to disappear under that bright red dome protecting them from the sun and rendering them headless; I watched as their two bodies, diminishing with increasing distance, were exposed for the first time to the eyes of the city. That was my last image of Soraya

Ângela alive. She was dressed all in white. Emilie had braided her hair, and the braids, tied with red ribbon, bounced on her shoulder blades. I remember noticing the mother-of-pearl scarab pinned to the collar of her organdy blouse. I don't know who gave it to her, but that pin, like almost anything new she was given, received much thoughtful contemplation. When the two came out of their room dressed and ready for their stroll, Soraya Ângela was craning her neck to get a good look at it, her chin glued to her collarbone, and the look in her almost-crossed eyes gave the impression of being drawn into herself. That's my last image of her from the front; minutes later, I watched as they faded into the distance, following the course of their one and only outing.

The next morning you burst into my room and shook me awake in my hammock. It took me a while to open my eyes and see you—a basket of flowers in your right hand, not crying yet or even shouting, just irritated at my sleepiness, that slackness we feel toward the world when we're waking up. Generally, when you came to my room it was because you wanted to hear some stories and look through my books of engravings, but then you'd have your brother with you and you wouldn't have a look in your eyes so wild as to blot out everything else. So I asked after your brother and you said, "It's her, the little girl, my cousin." You rummaged around in your basket nervously and your whole body was trembling, and when you covered your face with your hands it looked like flowers were blooming out of your eyes. The stammering, the hoarse whisper, the impossibility of saying her name out loud: "the little girl—she—my cousin" was all you could get out. I jumped up from my hammock and dashed to the next room, which was deserted: silence surrounded by four shadowy walls. Then a noise outside the room attracted my attention, a confusion of voices, horns, a hubbub. I ran to the terrace, saw the intense light in the street, and in the center of it Emilie kneeling down beside a small body covered by a sheet. There was nothing anyone could do: she wasn't even in her death throes, and before a lifeless body there's nothing to be done, not even grieve. Helplessness and an unwillingness to accept what happened enveloped us, and I suddenly thought to run down the hall and wake my brothers and tell them point-blank, maybe even with a bit of spite, that she was lying there in the middle of the street, all torn up. I knocked on their door and did just that, blurting out what had happened without waiting for their reaction, because if they weren't sensitive to life, they wouldn't be to death. Or if they were, I didn't care. When I walked back past my room, I noticed you were huddled in the hammock, eyes closed, your flowers scattered on the floor, and your arms buried in the basket. Down on the street, I found Emilie next to the public telephone, with your brother in her arms stroking Soraya's rag doll. Emilie looked calm in an odd sort of way, but her hands were trembling, and when she spoke her voice was very loud. She said the same thing several times, and it was her look more than her voice that told me she was talking to me, telling me to send Anastácia Socorro to the Parisian to get Samara Délia and Father. I suggested maybe we should call an ambulance to take Soraya to the hospital.

"Our people die at home, not in the hospital," said Emilie harshly. Then she asked me to lock up the store and hang the black satin draping, without Father having to get involved.

Father and Samara had been working together at the store for some time; having her there with him was a gesture of clemency on his part. They didn't talk much, and whenever I stopped in I was aware of the uneasiness between them. More than once he steered me into the hall between showcases and whispered, "Have you said hello to your sister yet?" or he'd ask how "the children" were doing—by which he meant you, your brother, and Soraya Ângela, the three "grandchildren" being raised as his sons and daughters.

When Soraya Ângela was first born, Father kept her at arm's length, as if she were a ghost or a forbidden toy. As time passed, the ghost took shape and the toy, forbidden or not, became attractive, enchanting even. A cautious closeness grew between the two. Not long before her death, Soraya had taken to preparing Father's pipe and bringing him his pistachios and almonds after coffee. Once she intercepted the maid and insisted that she be the one to deliver her grandfather's slippers. He thanked her, somewhat flustered and embarrassed, and remarked to Emilie, careful not to be overheard: "You know, she's not so bad after all. And she's got your eyes." In time, he allowed, even insisted, that Soraya and Samara Délia sit at the table with the family for dinner, and before long he was smiling at the child's antics as she acted out scenes from our walks around town. Father's growing affability toward Soraya Ângela enraged my brothers, who had to swallow their anger and hide their derisive snickers behind the feeble and inane expression of those who can give vent to neither anger nor laughter. Soraya Ângela knew she was an unwelcome presence, and that was her weapon, her triumph. Little by little she began filling the space of the house, attracting attention not by movement but by her very immobility. She'd plant herself in front of some object (the statue on the fountain, the clock in the parlor) and forget everything, everybody, maybe even herself. It was interesting how no one could remain indifferent to this. Sometimes I had the impression she would concentrate on something so that others would concentrate on her. Soraya provoked anger in some, impatience in others. I myself admit to a certain fascination and a boundless determination to isolate the facial features that would lead me to the identity of her father. Not even Emilie had managed to wrest this secret from her daughter; it remained inviolable, a dark box lost at the bottom of the sea. I remember whole portions of my brothers' adolescence were devoted to this quest. They went so far as to insinuate that Soraya's light hair might be chalked up to the frequent visits Samara Délia and I made to Dorner's. As soon as this got back to Dorner, he kept his distance from the family. Alluding to the incident in one of his letters from Germany, Dorner observed that slander is worshiped like a god in Amazonas. "It's the pinnacle of creativity in provincial life," he wrote, "in addition to being the only way for fools to endure the tedium. It is not, therefore, as absurd as it may seem to say that even fools can be creative."

Creativity being the brother of action, my brothers combed the downtown brothels, going from door to door showing Samara's picture to the old madams in the red-light district, asking if any of them knew their errant sister, the lunatic novice who might have slipped out of the family home at night, and as an answer received peals of laughter and pinches on the arm. Imagining this to be mockery, they went upstairs to the rooms, photograph in hand, and asked the twelve-year-old girls if they'd ever seen anyone resembling the girl in the picture, but no leads turned up, nothing, at least not in the houses downtown. Again and again they'd go out at dark and return only the next day, unsteady on their feet, snarling at Emilie and the maid, searching Samara Délia's room for some suspicious sign. Then they took to visiting the whorehouses tucked away in the jungle, and once they arrived home at dawn in a jalopy with two women and began blowing the horn and pounding on the door; when Emilie appeared on the upper terrace they asked, bellowing, if they could sleep with the women in their sister's room. Emilie lost her temper that time. She flew down the stairs and out the door in her lace nightgown with her

slipper in her hand, and took off after the bunch of
them, screaming, "You shameless hooligans!" and told
the boys they could take their bitches to the jungle to
sleep. Then she slammed the door in their faces, locked
up the house, and came back upstairs muttering under
her breath: "I never thought I'd know hell in this life."

My brothers were aghast and furious when Samara
Délia decided to move out of the house and live by herself at some distant and undisclosed location. Only
Emilie and Father knew where she'd gone. A few days
before leaving Manaus, I asked Emilie to take me to see
Samara, and she agreed. One Sunday night we set out
on foot and before long were standing in front of the
Parisian. I couldn't figure out why we would be stopping there on a Sunday night, unless Emilie wanted to
pick something up to bring to Samara Délia. Once we
stepped inside and the lights were turned on, I was enveloped in the quietness of Saturday afternoons—the
faint luminosity emanating from the huge glass showcases and even the objects (cloth, fans, vials of perfume) arranged on the shelves: an ambience recalling
fragments of images emerging and dissipating almost
simultaneously: an afternoon in pieces, or the one afternoon that was all the afternoons of childhood.

It never occurred to me that Samara Délia might be
living in the private room Emilie used to disappear into
after our Arabic lessons. Though not exceptionally large
in dimensions, the room seemed quite spacious because
it was almost empty and all the walls were white. The
great height of the ceiling made you forget it existed,

and lent less weight and presence to the body stretched out on the small bed. Her head was averted, but when she turned toward us I recognized the sadness one finds on expressionless faces. As soon as Emilie had gone, my sister stood and came to greet me. I felt as if I were embracing a stranger and an intimate at once, as if she had somehow split into the kid sister of a distant time and the mother of more recent days. For several minutes we didn't speak. Then I walked over to the table where I saw an open notebook, a calendar, and the picture of Soraya Ângela posing beside the statue. Samara noticed that I was looking at the photograph.

"It's the only one left," she said, and this phrase was the prelude to a brief conversation. She spoke carefully and stiffly. First she asked after Dorner, and when I told her he intended to go to Germany, she wanted to know the exact day he'd be leaving and whether or not he would be coming back. Then she enumerated some of her illusions and disillusionments, and announced that her other brothers' hostility no longer mattered to her.

"The persecution, the insults and threats, that was their way of punishing me; then I became a diversion for imbeciles."

What had most tormented her was the impossibility of ever having a conversation with her daughter. My sister didn't bemoan her fate or feel sorry for herself during the time they lived cloistered in her room. It was in the course of the second year, after mother and daughter had come downstairs and joined the life of the house, that Soraya's muteness emerged as a stigma.

Crying had been her early form of communication, but crying is the voice of someone who can't talk yet. As Soraya got older, there were only gestures, her lips moving, her face contorted, as her mother waited for the first word, the first sounds that would express life. During the last months of Soraya Ângela's life, my sister frequently woke in the middle of the night thinking she heard voices, conversations, but she'd find her daughter sleeping quietly at her side. She still dreamed, living here at the Parisian, but now she dreamed they were actually talking together, and in one brief dream Soraya did all the talking while her mother listened, incapable of saying a word.

"It feels as if my whole body is paralyzed," she confessed. "So I try to put off going to sleep, to avoid the nightmares."

I didn't dare ask questions. I listened attentively, watching her talk without raising her eyes from the photograph of her daughter standing beside the statue. I remember taking the picture from a distance, and the eight-by-twelve blowup accentuated this, the two faces losing some of their sharpness. The saffron-colored face of the statue was rendered a dark gray, in contrast to the lighter gray of Soraya Ângela's face, almost in profile. This image, which seemed somehow to give strength to my sister's voice, was the last flash of fire animating the sinner's lungs, removing the fear and guilt that envelops him the entire everlasting night.

During our visit together, what upset us most was recalling the years of silence, the period we spent alienated from each other. The subject was taboo, though we knew the long estrangement would mark us for the rest of our lives. I understood that Samara Délia was expecting some kind of remark or judgment from me, and my reaction was to consult my watch, pretending I was pressed for time. Then I thought of something that helped quiet my anxiety in the face of such a painful subject: as we had exchanged our few words and occasional glances, we had been drawing closer to one another, because silence too plays a part in the intimacy between two people. Maybe she didn't want to talk about it anymore; the fact that she was no longer looking at the photograph suggested a change in subject.

I looked around the room and noticed that the bed was the same one the two of them had slept in at the house. It was the single object common to the two homes, two lives, two eras. Samara went back to the bed, sat down, and remained quiet, as if waiting for a sign from me. For the first time our eyes met, and how many thoughts inhabited that lingering meeting. Who could ever untangle so many confused memories? Because our joined gaze contained a mingling of scenes and feelings scattered over distinct periods: riding the streetcar, diving into the freezing cold water of the igarapés, the secrets of siblings, the fear and jealousy that possessed one watching the other prepare for her first dance, and especially the smiles of complicity the times we were awakened by creaking bedsprings, muffled voices, and heavy breathing. Barely containing our giggles, we'd tiptoe out of our room and down the long hallway to our parents' door, where we'd stand guard like two sentinels, unable to see but our eager imaginations doing cartwheels, imagining what was going on in there. And, still laughing (one hand over our mouths, the other squeezing the other's hand), we'd press our ears to the door to hear not just creaking springs but a storm of laughter and other unidentifiable sounds: a circus of passion in the heart of the night. We were determined to stay right there as long as the fury of coupling bodies continued. Silence was a long time coming, and sometimes never came: sleepiness would triumph over curiosity, and we'd go back to our room like two sleepwalkers feeling our way down the hall. In the morning we'd wake to the sound of the vigorous footsteps and hand-clapping of a mother who seemed to have slept three straight nights.

I remember one day when the grown-ups were talking about Esmeralda and Américo's honeymoon, Emilie remarked:

"There's no such thing! Love's honey lasts into old age and only dries up when we die."

All the years I lived at home, Emilie lived up to that remark. She suffered the death of loved ones and the sorrows of the whole family, and still managed to make each night a festival of pleasure that infected all the rooms of both houses she lived in, without worrying about what the child in the next bedroom or the maid in the back room was going to say or think, so that if tedium and despondency wore her down, the nights of loving restored her vigor and her hunger for life. And that was how my sister and I discovered that our parents were extravagant both in disagreement and in love.

Our complicity, which seemed peculiar to nighttime, came to light when memory waded into the waters of childhood. I looked at Samara and wondered what vestiges remained of that other person, the child Samara. A residue of those early days could be seen in her eyes, but the smiles and antics were gone, and her voice had changed as well. Slow and calm without being austere, halfway between a question and an assertion, the voice said: "You were the one who had the organdy flowers made; it was either you or the others—who?" I didn't know who had sent the garland of delicately embroidered imitation orchids to cover Soraya Ângela's head. But that was what was on my sister's mind. She was trying to disentangle a whole web of mysteries and I couldn't clarify what was for me at best uncertain; nor was I interested in nourishing suspicions. I let the question hang in the air, until our silence erased it. I could see that Samara Délia was upset and dissatisfied with my reticence. I was the one who had initiated the visit, and here I'd hardly opened my mouth. Finally, feeling eager to leave, I asked why she had decided to come live at the Parisian, a place full of shadows of the past.

"Your past, not mine," she said sharply. "I left my whole life behind in the other house, in the room where I suffered for years. I decided to live here because Father's silence is terrifying; it's almost a challenge."

"He doesn't talk to you? Not a word?"

"He talks to me as you'd talk to a mirror, and he spends hours on end reading the Book in an undertone. His voice is hardly audible, and I don't understand a word of what I do hear. I have the impression that he reads in order to forget me."

She walked me to the door. Her eyes were moist, and in the same calm voice she said she'd rather he rail at her or haul off and slap her.

"Nothing could hurt more than his silence," she said, on the verge of tears, hugging me goodbye. And the body that was hugging me was no longer adolescent.

THE RETURN

OUR MOTHER'S HOUSE was barely five hundred yards from Emilie's. Along the short walk between the two houses, I was excited to find certain areas intact, frozen in time, as if nothing new had been built since we lived there. Not a single wall or column seemed to be missing from the most ancient buildings, and the stone lions, the wild boar, and the bronze Diana were still posed in their places in the square, surrounded by acacias and park benches where people reclined to contemplate the stained-glass tiles on the bandstand or the iguanas and alligators heading for the edge of the lake, attracted by shadows of herons and jabiru who slept or pretended to sleep balanced on thin, thin stalks that disappeared in the water. Here was the bench, halfway between the bandstand and the two huge bronze sentinels, where the Sicilian brothers used to sit jabbering back to back, until without a pause in their chatter they'd stand up simultaneously and walk in opposite directions, escorted by a pack of mangy dogs. The brothers' rag-doll heads flopped down toward the ground, and they always wore army boots, collarless shirts. Anyone who followed them as they traipsed around town had to admit to a certain admiration for their intricate route as they wound through deserted alleys, bursting into abandoned houses that disfigured the whole block, and found themselves at the end of the street (and the city) at a low wall of pinkish rocks where all the curses of the world were inscribed in whitewash and charcoal. Then, each taking his own path back, they'd arrive in the square at the same moment, sit down on the same bench, and resume a conversation that had begun God knows when. Each one's back served as leaning post for the other, and the dogs nipped at their boots, shredding the bottom of their pants, while the soldiers posted beside the bronze likenesses of soldiers laughed and pointed.

Nothing that lived and breathed in the square remained from those days, however. Oh, the monuments were the same, but the twins' bench looked like a marooned tombstone. Gazing at the trees, the lake, the bridge, and the paths circling that mirror of water, I missed the darting silhouettes of animals and their unmistakable racket.

Passing through the iron gate to Emilie's house, I was equally surprised by the absence of shrill bird and monkey calls and the bleating of the sheep. The front door was locked. Peeking through one of the ornamental slits cut in the wall, I looked down the deserted hallway and straight through to the smaller patio with its trellis and litter of dry leaves and a tiny edge of the back patio. Everything about the house seemed to be asleep, and when I knocked on the door and shouted several times for Emilie, there was no answer in the stillness. Then I remembered the maid saying Emilie would probably be on her way home from the market, and pictured her carrying a basket full of fruit and vegetables and fish just like the long-ago morning when they scattered on the gray paving stones now covered by asphalt, so that I couldn't be sure of the spot where Soraya's body had lain broken. I stood there near the jambo tree a few minutes, overwhelmed by indecision. I stared at the pink blossoms covering the branches, the purplish fruit rotting on the grass, and longed for the smell of the white jasmine, which the grown-ups called Saman, perfume from another time, the fragrance of childhood.

So I decided to wander the city, communing with my long absence, and return to the house at lunchtime. As soon as I crossed the metal bridge over the igarapé and entered the narrow streets of an unfamiliar neighborhood, I was met by the gaudy colors of the wooden houses, a strong, acrid smell, and the singsong voices of street kids, their faces cutouts in the window holes, at the very border between inside and outside, but it was as if the border itself (a warped and colorless frame) meant nothing to those faces staring into space, strangers to the passing of time and the passersby trying carefully, deliberately, to take it all in. There were other moments when the faces stared back at me urgently, making me feel shy and a little scared, and even with the abyss that existed between us, the strangeness was mutual, and likewise the fear. I didn't want to feel like an intruder, having been born and grown up here. I was trying to wander aimlessly, but there were no parallel streets; the design was a confused geometry, and the river, always the river, was the point of reference, instead of the square and the church spire of our neighborhood.

I spent the entire morning in the city forbidden to us as children, where there were duels between drunken men, where the women were either thieves or prostitutes, where blades sharpened on machetes were used to carve men as well as beasts. We grew up on sordid and macabre stories about that child-killing neighborhood, inhabited by beings from the other world, the sad refuge of monsters. I would have to distance myself from everything and everyone I knew in order to exorcise those monsters of the imagination, to truly cross the bridge and reach the space denied us: sludge and standing water, wooden slats painted all the colors of the rainbow with vertical and horizontal chinks between them allowing us to peer inside: swarms of dirty, naked children, squatting under a sinuous canopy of colorful hammocks, where, encircled by flies, women suckled their babies or fanned charcoal fires, and always the smells of frying, of fish caught virtually alongside the house.

After my labyrinthine tour of the neighborhood, I decided to go back downtown by another route; I wanted to take a canoe from the igarapé out onto the Negro River and watch from a distance as Manaus slowly detached itself from the sun, a dim mass of rock revealing its first outlines, growing wider and more detailed with each stroke of the oar. But the passage through a diffuse landscape before a wavering slate-gray horizon interrupted by scattered glass and steel towers seemed to be taking as long as an ocean crossing; it seemed as though I'd been in the boat a very long time. I got the impression rowing was a futile act: it added up to remaining indefinitely in the middle of the river. Meanwhile, those two verbs—to row and to remain—erased the opposition between movement and immobility. And the closer we drew to the port, the more insistently I remembered what you used to say: "A city is different seen from a distance, over the water. It's not even a city. It lacks perspective, depth, design, and, most important, a human presence, the vital core of the city. Maybe it's simply a plane, an incline, or various planes and inclines forming imprecise angles with the surface of the water."

It took a while, in real time, for us to tie up at the dock. The sun, almost directly overhead, beat down mercilessly. It was difficult to open my eyes, not due to the brightness (that was a problem) but, rather, because everything was too visible. My eyes open, I woke up to the nearly twenty years I'd been away. The distance from the port proper to the boats bobbing at their moorings was much greater and the walk between them introduced me to the horrors of a Manaus I didn't recognize: a filthy stretch of beach littered with the scraps of human misery and filled with a stench that emanated from the ground, from the slime, from the bowels of the red rocks and the insides of the boats. I was walking on a sea of garbage with everything else you can think of mixed in: fruit rinds, tin cans, bottles, the skeletons of canoes and animals. A great profusion of vultures eagerly picked through the debris washed up during high tide as well as worm-eaten objects that had lain buried for months, centuries perhaps. Apart from the heat, I was irritated by the groups skirmishing and grunting absurd noises as they tried out some phrase, maybe in English: seedy tour guides whose mutilated bodies and deformed faces bound them to this oozing wasteland, this piece of the city writhing like raw flesh engulfed in flames.

I paid the boatman and fled the uproar, the entreaties, the shouts, the strident voice of an invisible loudspeaker announcing the boats' departures, home ports, and destinations, strange towns with strange sounds in their names, seemingly senseless names the tongue could hardly pronounce, but that nevertheless existed, not necessarily on maps but in people's lives, places where somebody lived. The beach ended in a cluster of shacks, a maze of wood stretching on down the sidewalk and into the street. Laid out for sale on cardboard boxes were statues of saints and scapulars, drawings of a green dragon being pierced by the lance of a saint on horseback, manta rays and toucans striated by the texture of the wood, miniature anacondas, tiny bikinis, bracelets, necklaces, and earrings. What attracted me most were the masks made of bark, wrinkled and shriveled by the sun, wizened like human skin. Crouched in their shacks full of merchandise, these people probably didn't imagine that not so long ago their ancestors had worn similar masks. Battered by time and by violence, the faces and masks seemed to belong to the same bodies, bodies indifferent to everything, even the curiosity they aroused in the tourists circling in search of some cooling shade or clutching their cameras with lenses powerful enough to capture an illusive contact with reality.

On the highest part of the sloping square, just in front of the church doors, a spectacle burst the midday torpor. The man came out of nowhere. From a distance, he resembled a Faunus. He stood out so clearly in that sea of humidity that I decided to walk a few steps closer. Coiled around his outstretched arms, neck, and torso was a boa constrictor; a parrot perched on either shoulder, and the rest of his body swarmed with tiny monkeys who didn't seem to mind the presence of the snake in the least and were attached to cords fastened around his wrists, ankles, and neck. When he took his first step, he looked like a small tree dropping its leaves: the monkeys' jumping became feverish, the boa rippled in his arms, and the parrots' wings flapped madly. Just then the church bells rang to proclaim noon, a weighty clanging that reverberated in the noise on the street, creating a strange harmony, a whirlwind of dissonance, a festival of sounds. I remember wishing you were there beside me to see that walking wonder explode in the middle of the luminous glare, cutting through the curtain of oppressive heat.

The human shrub filled the square, attracting passersby, freeze-framing shopkeepers as they locked their doors, and transfixing the faithful on their way out of church who crossed themselves as they hurried to join the others. A flood of law students descended the steps and streamed through the gates to stand beside tourists crouched down, one eye to the viewfinder, cameras cocked. Some of them inched forward on their knees or climbed up into trees to surprise the shrub from on high: seen from above, perhaps the man would disappear, or at least his head might blur behind the twisting ropes and animals. I kept changing positions, moving closer and then farther away, trying to get a glimpse of his face. I'd like to describe him down to the last detail, but descriptions always distort things. Besides, the invisible can't be transcribed, it must be invented. A pictorial image would do it more justice. A palette knife and paints, masses of color worked with quick, incisive movements, might capture something appearing among the curls of hair and vines that ended in the tangle of cords. Though his only clothing consisted of a strip of cloth between his legs, almost no skin could be seen; a crust of dirt formed a kind of grimy carapace over his body. I was surprised not to see a gourd or can or some kind of container for alms; but this was no beggar, or at least not one like the others in town. Even so, after getting a good close-up, hopefully at the right angle to catch his peculiar gait, the tourists insisted on throwing coins and paper money at him: the price of perpetuating a vision of the outlandish. But it was the children who pressed forward to scoop up the booty, while the man continued down the hill, arms open wide, coordinating a double movement: his body moving forward and the animals moving on his body. He was distancing himself from the crowd, amid loud laughter and curses, pelted with spitballs, hunks of bread, and stones, which struck the monkeys, grazed a parrot's wing, or bounced off the coiling snake. The successive impacts produced a muffled storm of thudding sounds and a flurry of grunts, the only form of protest to the rain of garbage aimed at animals imprisoned in a cage without bars. But it was enough of a reaction to unleash a furious new salvo of missiles, in addition to threats, insults, and whoops of laughter. The man slowed his pace, stopping occasionally to regain his balance, trembling from top to bottom, but confident of his stability, his rootedness on the slanted ground, as if each step of his bare feet were tugging a taproot from deep in the earth. The volley of objects continued, with soldiers, longshoremen, street vendors, fishermen joining in. By that time the cameras were really whirring, radiant cyclopes doing pirouettes, because now the crowd was almost as outlandish as the human shrub, having progressed from contemplation to harassment to castigation and assault, to the point that I was a little scared, not of the man and his animals but of the crazed multitude, inflamed with hate under the midday sun. This wandering uproar filtered through the narrow paths between market stalls—passageways that moved and changed, created, destroyed, and modified by the hour with the appearance of new booths, permanent or roving: women and men and children carrying boxes and trays like an ant colony spreading out across the square. The crowd blundered on through the tight streets like an avalanche, curiously unable to, or uninterested in, stopping the man in his course: they seemed to want him alive and in motion with the animals, maybe in the hope that he'd become unsteady on his feet and the whole menagerie would inevitably totter and fall, the animals dismembering from the body and the body dismembered by the animals. Perhaps that was the challenge, the purpose, of this entertainment, but as far as my eyes could follow him he remained intact, only slowing his steps as he came to the top of a pile of red stones. Then he vanished in the sea of mud alongside the boats and the water. A wall of people took over the ramp and formed a dense and unstable cloud through which the shapes of keels and a diffuse black and greenish mass were visible.

A gray splotch suddenly appeared on the horizon, contrasting with the sheet of water; in seconds the splotch darkened, blending with the surface of the river, and that distant point seemed in broad daylight to anticipate the night, the way scattered areas on the horizon were blocked out by bluish clouds. A warm gust of wind made dust and paper swirl into eddies and threatened the fragile architecture of the wooden stalls, which swayed with their trinkets, provoking a sudden scurrying of previously invisible people, now madly trying to protect masks and other objects exposed to the wind; the pedestrian bridges over the mud creaked with the weight and agitation of all the people running to try to save the fruits and vegetables from the impending downpour.

I would have remained at the high end of the square a bit longer, watching the metamorphosis of the area and the people dashing to and fro, stalls and boats trying to fight the fury of nature, roofs and awnings creating new vistas on the ground and in the water, but I felt as though I'd already witnessed that scene, like someone who wakes up surprised to have been dreaming a dream from a previous night. In any case, I couldn't remember the place or time frame this image came from. There, before me, between the end of the square and the riverbank, a world of colors and motion (colors *in* motion) had transformed the dock into an enormous movable stage.

I thought I was the only spectator, attentive first to a boat lost between clouds and water, then to a caravan of longshoremen, then to the confusion of colorful keels. I'm not sure if I noticed or simply intuited that I wasn't alone in relishing that lively scene. You can't imagine how surprised I was to sense the approach of an obvious foreigner, someone clearly neither a tourist nor a local, extremely tall, dressed all in white, with a kind of ungainly walk, as if he needed something to lean on. It seemed he would walk straight up to me, but instead stopped a few steps away, his eyes still on the river; every so often he raised his head and turned to look for I don't know what. When I saw the gray hair and long, bony fingers, then I was sure it was him. He was staring at me, too, maybe because he'd noticed my excitement, but those beady blue eyes, practically glued to thick lenses, didn't recognize me yet. I continued gazing into his eyes, savoring for a moment the privacy of my recognition. Then I blurted, loud and clear, the two lines of German you always came back from class declaiming in that now distant cellar of adolescence. I've cultivated, ever since, the pleasure of reciting words and sounds that are unintelligible to me. Hearing my botched rendition, his face lit up, as if words themselves could dissolve the bitterness of a formerly serene countenance. He opened his arms and said: *"Du hier, Mädchen?"* and just stood there, arms flung wide, incredulous, his smile and his eyes trying to reconcile emotion and astonishment, oblivious to the sheets of paper cascading from his briefcase and scattering in the wind. Suddenly the rain came crashing down, shooting shrapnel at the city, roiling the waters of the river with its million splinters. Torn between the euphoria of our meeting and the fury of the storm, we were unsure where to seek shelter. He pointed to The River Mermaid, a bar near the wharf, but the rain had already nearly obscured everything on the horizon, engulfing the wharf and the port, and enveloping the city in mystery and reclusiveness. We broke into a run without agreeing on a destination and by the time we climbed the stairs and entered the church I could feel that my clothes were stuck to my body. Our footsteps, the water running off us onto the floor, our breathing—everything seemed to echo in that dark sanctuary lit only by chandeliers high up near the ceiling and the dozens of candles clustered around the feet of the statues, which made the saints look as if they were walking on flames. Heading down the center aisle, I studied the few visible alcoves of that dark, unfamiliar place. The rain, striking the roof of the nave above our heads, made a furious and incessant chatter.

WE STOPPED IN front of a side altar to the right of the central nave and sat on a dingy yellow marble step. This recessed area was lit by clumps of white candles, some enormous and others mere stubs of wax that had been lit who knows how long ago; together they formed a miniature landscape, a chain of hillocks surrounding the base of the statue. The flames grew as they neared the saint's feet, and the aureole of fire from tallest candles, perhaps lit that very morning, licked his plaster mantle and seemed still to be watching over the most recent prayers and entreaties. The dimness suggested a conversation in low voices. Dorner spoke very softly, almost in a whisper; he modulated his voice as the rain struck the roof with ever more intensity. He seemed short of breath occasionally, his head and upper body heaving as he inhaled, and mopped his sweaty face with a handkerchief. There was a certain anguish in this gesture, which served as a pause when he touched on delicate subjects. In brushstrokes that bounded over years, he told me something of his long stay in Manaus. His reserve made it easy for me to remain silent about my own life. Whenever I saw a certain look of curiosity in his eyes, I'd hurry to ask a question, picking up on some detail that had escaped elaboration. But in trying to sidestep his curiosity, I ended up heading down unwelcome paths in his life. Talking about certain things constitutes unmasking a belief, violating someone else's secret. In order to break the silence and avoid a revelation, we turned to our friends' stories. He enumerated deaths and absences: our neighbors from Minho, the Italian twins, compatriots of his I'd never met; and he became very animated remembering Uncle Hakim. (Little did we know he was at that moment en route to Manaus.) But his excitement was short-lived, and the insistent smile of bygone days never bloomed on his face. A hint of alienation and general disillusionment showed in the way he kept taking his glasses off and on, wiping his face with the handkerchief, tensing his body at each inhalation. At some point I noticed that he was also playing with his briefcase, which looked more like a leather satchel containing the accumulated relics and misfortunes of an entire life. From the large pile of notebooks and books he pulled out a sheet of white paper and a Faber pencil. With a sidelong glance I watched as he began writing almost dead-center and, wavering, struggled toward the edge of the page. He was copying out the lines I'd just recited. Then he scribbled some scattered words in Portuguese, and their position on the page seemed somewhat fortuitous: a tiny sky dotted with gray stars, forming a dense web of words that grew indistinct at times, because the fine-point mechanical pencil drew invisible letters, colorless wrinkles, watermarks. Then suddenly the angle at which the pencil was being held or the friction on the paper made the grayish loops and spirals come to life again, creating sharp and unexpected transitions from invisible to legible.

It was curious the way the grooves and scratches were concentrated on one part of the paper, so that only half of the white rectangle was ravaged by marks, as if some chaotic design formed an inner boundary within the boundaries of the rectangle. In that one area words proliferated like a blast of fireworks—words rearranged, phrases or parts of phrases inverted or modified—until the moment his hand stopped in midair and the pencil was set down on the marble.

He contemplated the page at length and, before handing it to me, asked—with an irony masquerading as humility and seriousness—that I supply the appropriate tone and cadence. As I read the lines, trying to follow the course by which he had come to the definitive version, he lit a cigarette and considered the altar of candles. I held the paper up and announced that nothing need be added or crossed out, and how strange it felt that now, after all these years, those two lines were no longer an entertainment for my ears, a game in an unfamiliar language; I knew that from that moment on, every time I recited the couplet to myself, I would have a premonition and hear Dorner's translation in my head, like a shadow alive and full of images. And I would never forget the graphic configuration of the words concentrated in the middle of the rectangle. The image that had been fixed in my mind was that of a comet diagonally crossing white space. Without taking his eyes off the statue with its feet in flames, Dorner said:

"That's a useful image to describe a translation: the tail of a comet following close behind the comet. At some indeterminate moment, the tail seems to want to find its own gravity, to become separate enough to be attracted by another heavenly body and yet always remain magnetized to its parent body; the comet and its tail, the original and the translation, the extremity that touches the head of the body, the beginning and end of the same journey. . . ."

His eyes turned to mine and he added in a joking, almost laughing, tone:

"Or of the same dilemma."

As soon as he said it, he assumed the same melancholy air, the gloomy expression, of someone who is languishing. Once again I thought of you, of your reports about the Dorner I barely knew, who gave you German lessons and talked on and on about photography, or Leipzig, or Berlin as seen by Kleist, about the war and the Germans persecuted and treated badly even here in Manaus. You'd visit me in the conservatory in the late afternoon; your tongue itching with stories, you'd tell the piano teacher a story from the life of Mahler and ask her to play Schubert's "Death and the Maiden," and before the minor movements were over you'd be asleep in your chair, your lips slack, dreaming that tomorrow maybe he would tell you the one about the saint buried in a little church in Hungary, martyred during the Roman occupation, whose body was discovered intact, the smile before he drew his last breath still visible on his face. The lives of the saints, the building of the great cathedrals, piles of stones glorifying the skies of Europe, and the volatile geography of Germany—all this as part of the German lessons he taught standing before a wrinkled map hung on the damp basement wall. I felt that looking at me, Dorner was trying to see you. He wanted you sitting there beside him, as he sketched scenes from the past, interpreting the poems of the German writer who, in his view, was closest to the image of God.

At this point I began nervously consulting my watch. I heard a single bell toll the first hour of afternoon and was startled by the passage of sixty minutes; the flow of time is so slow here that life can crawl along unhurriedly. But I felt pressed, not just by the simple desire to be free of Dorner but because remaining there alone with him meant surrendering to a boundless nostaglia. The couplet, his melancholy air, and, most of all, the silence—weren't these all subtle ways of evoking an impossible presence? Because it seemed that everything he said, or could have said, was addressed to you and plunged him into the past.

We walked down the side aisle, rain no longer drumming on the roof above us. Suddenly Dorner broke the silence. "Be careful not to step on the Lord's slaves," he said, peering down at the floor but continuing to walk. Accustomed by now to the dark, our eyes could just make out the bodies sleeping the sleep of death, shapes scattered in corners, hidden in shadowy niches. My thoughts were scattered, in total disarray, as I followed Dorner like a sleepwalker. I thought about your antipathy toward this place, your courageous and uncomplaining decision to go away for so long, as if distance might help you to forget, to exorcise the horror of these vagrants hidden from the world, destined to suffer among saints and oracles, witnesses to an insensible agony that threatens nothing and no one: the misery of simply waiting, the triumph of passivity and mute despair. I also thought about Dorner, an ascetic inhabitant of an isolated city, stubbornly offering philosophy classes to a ghost public, obsessed by the aroma of orchids, fleshy-leaved herbs, and androgynous flowers. He had lived a long time among books and the plant world, and could name from memory three thousand plants. I have no way of knowing whether the solitude bothered him or whether there was anything morbid in his decision to settle here, listening to his own voice, conversing with the Other that is he himself: perverse, transparent, fragile complicity. The few times you've mentioned Dorner in the intervening years, you referred not to a human being but a "mysterious character," an "enigmatic survivor of a shipwreck whom chance had landed at the confluence of two great rivers, arriving like a drop of dew appearing imperceptibly on the skin of a dark petal at some unknown moment during the night." You and your passion for making a lie of the world and the people in it, creating and annotating illusions in your refuge on rua Montseny or in the sordid bowels of "Chinatown," deep in the nocturnal heart of Barcelona, all to prove that distance is an antidote to the real and the visible world. Unlike you, I was never able to run away from it all. I became so well versed in reality, you know where I ended up: trapped between the four walls of hell.

I said goodbye to Dorner knowing I would never see him again. As I hurried off, I bumped into a lot of people, fruit vendors, childhood friends, all of them wanting to know your whereabouts. What could I tell them? That for a long time your letters arrived with postmarks from all over Europe? How could I possibly explain to these people your mad fascination with Gaudí, or the poem you dedicated to the Holy Family, or the strange flavor of orgeat, or dawn in Lloret del Mar? It was easier to tell them you were on your way, or that one day you would come back; and so I sidestepped the truth, claiming urgent business and not bothering to hide the weariness and exasperation of someone come from afar who already feels like going back. As I walked I became more and more agitated, because I couldn't stop constantly consulting my watch and I didn't know why, since it was completely unnecessary and made moving through the crowd even more difficult.

Maybe I was trying to postpone seeing Emilie, to stay away from the homestead that much longer, or to avoid as much as possible the unmistakable terrain of our childhood. I suppose that's why, almost without noticing, I had strolled through downtown, when I could have shortened my route considerably by cutting through the street between the church and the house. I walked fast, not because I was really in a hurry but because I felt like fleeing, as if haste were a shield against the crowd that blocked the sidewalks and the entrance to the house like a fallen tree.

Opening a path through the crowd, I saw Hindié appear and run toward me, all in black, dark shocks of hair falling to her shoulders. Arms flung open, she was crying and shouting something incomprehensible, two burning tears streaming down her wet face. I took her desperate and dramatic gestures to mean that I shouldn't go in the house, that I should get out of there, that all was lost. Hindié threw her opulent body on mine; we stood, embracing, on the far side of the street, and between sobs I could hear the furious heart-beat of a woman who had just lost a friend of fifty years. I don't know how I managed to stay on my feet, even as paralyzed as I was, with a body as immense as hers draped over me. But we stood for a long time under the hot sun until finally I backed away and into our house, where I found the maid with her face swollen, babbling fragments of phrases: your mother, your grandmother. . . .

The child and her doll were sitting on the swing in the middle of the yard staring at one another. I went up to my room and thought about Hindié, how the way she acted had stopped me from going inside the house already plunged into mourning. Why bother crossing the street, if beyond that gate what prevailed was the murmuring of curiosity and grief, so many people bleary-eyed in the face of death?

It was painful not to see Emilie, painful to resign myself to the impossibility of seeing her after having postponed this trip so many times, caught in the net of dailiness, at every year's end thinking: it's time for a visit, time to satisfy this longing, time to curl up with her in the arc of the hammock. I hadn't heard from her for several years, but Hindié would have been following her life step by step. Once the last of the children had moved out, Emilie decided to live alone, even to the point of asking Anastácia Socorro to do the same. The old family laundress returned to the interior, though she always came back for the birthday luncheons that gathered the family together. Emilie often told Hindié that solitude and old age are supports for one another, and that an old person who lives alone takes refuge in the past, which is vast and not infrequently gratifiying.

All the rooms in the house were in perfect order, a

lace coverlet on each bed, hammocks hung diagonally in each room dividing the space, and the Kasher and Esfahan carpets dignifying the living room where the black clock stood. Emilie nurtured a vague hope that one day someone would come from very far away to share her solitude. Hindié told me that Emilie must have had a premonition of my arrival, because she'd been talking about us a lot, and once, referring to you, she said: "That dear boy had to cross the ocean and live on another continent in order to be able to come home one day." She also talked to herself, carrying on conversations in a foreign language even with the animals, and lately she had been waking up in the wee hours and opening the windows to stare out at the unreal horizon in memory formed by villages wedged into the mountainsides of a distant country. And one morning Hindié walked into the kitchen to find the table covered with delicacies Emilie had prepared all through the night. Hindié assumed the children or grandchildren were coming for a party that day, but Emilie informed her it was just in homage to those of her people at the other side of the world. "I smelled the aroma of the sea and of figs, and suspected my relatives there were calling me," she said.

One day Emilie got it into her head to summon Expedito to dig out the offerings packed away in the maids' quarters, and after that she spent days and days dusting them off and stroking each one with her fingertips; then she asked him to read the names and origins of the donors. Until the Friday she died, there were people who looked in on her, and the ones who came that morning saw she was near the end and made a point of getting out the news, which spread through town like a hurricane.

Hindié visited her friend every morning at seven o'clock. When she arrived that Friday, Hindié had thought it odd, as I had, that the house was so silent, the animals quiet, the doors shut tight. Hindié always carried her rosary beads and the keys to the house tucked inside her corset. She let herself in the side gate and even before reaching the back patio had a premonition of impending death. "The animals didn't even stir when I came in the yard," she said. It seemed as if all eyes were one eye, united by an enormous melancholy.

Hindié let out a scream when she noticed one slate deeper red than the others; the stain directly beneath the foot of one of the stone angels was still spreading. She called to Emilie, noticing that the wide bedroom window overlooking the patio was closed up tight, and only later discovered two parallel red streaks and found the turtle Sálua scratching at the kitchen door. Apparently the only animal still alive, Sálua had some red stains on his shell; there were drips and splotches spattering the kitchen sink and on the floor, which Hindié followed down the hall to the telephone stand. Emilie was motionless, almost lifeless, the telephone cord coiled around her neck and in her hair; her right hand cupped the receiver and her left shielded her eyes.

I remember hearing the phone ring two or three times early that morning before I went out, and being startled. Maybe that had been Emilie's last call for help, her way of finding me to say goodbye.

Panic and anguish in the face of death, the house swept by a windstorm, an earthquake in the heart of the family—she didn't know whom to turn to on this morning outside time, the house in ruins, all upside down, where prayers mingle with confessions, as if holy words had the power to prohibit the absence, the emptiness left by death. Shaken and scared, Hindié walked through the house shouting the names of everyone she could think of and lurched up the stairs to open all the bedroom doors, forgetting that Emilie lived alone and that only she, Hindié, visited her each morning. When she came back downstairs, her hands were shaking so much it was difficult to unwind the telephone cord from Emilie's neck and untangle it from her hair. Chattering to herself nonstop, Hindié dragged Emilie into the living room, lay her down on the sofa, and placed a cushion under her bloody head. Her own hands and face were covered with blood by the time she went back to the phone and checked the list of frequently used telephone numbers. She called Hector Dorado's house but he couldn't understand a word she was saying and hung up, figuring she was just some lunatic or a kid playing a prank; in her panic Hindié had switched into Arabic, which was no more than gibberish to the doctor. Next, she called Uncle Emílio, who immediately recognized her voice as well as the language she was speaking. Nearly out of her mind, all she could do at first was to mumble a prayer as she nervously fingered her rosary beads. The prayer was familiar to Uncle Emílio, though it did seem strange to be hearing it so early in the morning and over the telephone. He had to raise his voice to jog Hindié out of her prayer and into the horrible news. From then on there was a whole network of crossed lines: the telephone rang off the hook and no one even thought to wipe the blood off until Yasmine arrived and was put in charge of incoming and outgoing calls.

Uncle Emílio arrived before the doctor. He brought two sisters from the Holy Home of Mercy with him, who administered first aid, to no avail. Remember those nuns who came to the house sometimes after novenas? (One time Emilie scolded you because you kept trying to reach the crucifix gleaming on the front of each black habit with your toy shovel.) The nuns wanted to take Emilie to the hospital, but Hector arrived and, after examining her head wound and taking her blood pressure, buried his face in the couch cushion beside Emilie's head.

"He didn't want to cry in front of the others," said Hindié.

The doctor was the only one who stayed with the body. Later Emilie's Manaus local sons arrived with their wives and children. They walked past the sofa as if tentatively crossing a bridge, gazing down fearfully at the silent face sunken into the cushion, and for the first time didn't find those two bright and benevolent eyes of the woman they always pretended to hate. Because in that very instant of tension and pain, a son,

encountering the silence of the mother, begins himself
to age. For a few seconds they stared at the motionless
body stretched out on the sofa and then withdrew from
the rest of the family to seek refuge in the backyard.
Only there, protected by a curtain of greenery, could
they sob and cry, their faces hidden from strangers'
eyes. Their weeping was not merely a reaction to the
end of a life; it was also the result of the terrible and
belated revelation that their lives had been a succession
of mediocre and shameful acts, the whole while they
depended on that dying woman—they, who couldn't
bear to witness Emilie's or anyone's last agony, and
who had only come to visit her when they lacked some
material comfort. Hindié knew all this because she was
one of Emilie's few confidantes, maybe the only one in-
timately familiar with daily life at the house long before
those two went off on their own.

When I talked to Uncle Hakim that evening, I understood how profoundly affected he had been by
Hindié's smell; it was as if she used that unmistakable
smell to imprint on people the memory of the past that
she emitted from every pore of her monumental body. I
wouldn't know how to describe or compare the strange
aroma that hovered around her like a halo, invisible but
inseparable from her body, but it was a bit like the
smell of candle wax that permeated the shadowy atmosphere of the church where I'd talked with Dorner:
the odor spreading through the nave, linking the
church with my memories. Hindié had been living with
that strange smell for many years, so rooted in her body

that it announced her presence, like the echo of foot-steps that tells us someone will appear at any moment before our eyes.

But it wasn't just smell that was peculiar to Hindié Conceição that morning she came rushing to meet me in the street. The somber dress, the timbre of her voice, her hands yanking at her curly hair, her lips vanishing inside her mouth as if she'd swallowed them, the long moments of silence—all this was part of the ritual of mourning. Her pain and sorrow were clear in her wild gestures, a kind of boldness to keep her from fading away, or fading away after her friend's death. I refused to keep wake over Emilie's body, but I listened as Hindié described events and conversations; she spoke in a rather restrained voice, waved her arms a lot, and when her eyes became red and streaked she got up out of her chair and came to me with hugs and kisses. Those big eyes were still burning on Sunday, and that messy, yellowing hair seemed to lend her face a torment very near despair.

HINDIÉ

OT JUST EMILIE'S friends, but anyone who
wanted to know anything about her came to
talk to me; they knew I was like a sister to her. Some
brought bouquets of flowers, filling the place with the
fragrance of an anticipated sadness, because there on
the sofa Emilie was still breathing, though the shadow
of death hung over her. With all the white flowers and
greenery, the telephone calls and messages of condolence, it was as if the burial vault had been brought inside the house.

And there was something else that bothered me: the
presence of those two insolent sons. They didn't come
talk to me, they didn't so much as touch Emilie, not

even once; it was as if she were a statue lying there.
When they were teenagers, I remember, everyone was
always furious with them; they got themselves ex-
pelled from every school in town, and the priests often
punished them harshly, like making them kneel on a
mound of husked corn in the hot sun from high noon
until the first star of evening appeared. Emilie never
seemed to lose patience, she put up with all their non-
sense, but one day their father got so mad he tied
them to the living-room table and left them there
alone, like dumb animals with no masters, until Emilie finally convinced him to untie them. She didn't always show such restraint, however; sometimes when
they were tied up and complained of hunger she'd go
to them before his pardon had been decreed, and then
all hell would break loose because it seemed as if it
were all her fault: their rebellion, their hatred, their
lack of discipline. They never said a word to me,
maybe because I was friends with Samara, whom their
father considered a rare flower and doted on without
realizing it, or at least without most other people realizing it.

It's hard to determine the cause of a child's rebellion, especially the kind of precocious delinquency, the
envy and violence, that possessed those two from very
early on. They made a pact against their sister, in spite
of the fact that ever since Soraya Ângela's birth, and
particularly since her death, Emilie had been begging
them to stop persecuting their sister and leave her in
peace; she pleaded with her sons as one might plead

with a criminal or dangerous fugitive, destined to die in a house of no escape. But then they'd paid no attention to their father's request either, when years before his death he'd gathered all the men of the house and asked the only son literate in Arabic to read and translate a verse from the sura on women. He wanted all three to understand that according to the word of God the Compassionate there was always pardon and clemency. Admitting that Samara had been born and raised before a clouded mirror, he explained that a woman who has fallen into sinfulness may repent by meditating alone in a room closed to the light of the sun and to all other eyes for five days and five nights. But even this failed to make them the least bit tolerant of their sister; in fact, the only result seemed to be increased disdain for their father for having used a sacred text to pardon the unpardonable.

Not only did they continue tormenting Samara, but they effectively banished her from the family and swore to create a scandal if she so much as stepped outside the house or used the family name. And until recently they were still snorting around like wild animals searching for a clue to her hideaway. They did eventually find out that she was living at the Parisian, but as long as your grandfather was alive they didn't dare bother her, because they knew they'd find themselves flat broke if they so much as set foot in the store to threaten their sister. The old man protected her tooth and nail; toward the end of his life he seemed more concerned about Samara than about

Emilie. I heard he brought her flowers and planted little fruit trees in the tiny yard out back of the store,
and one day he even went to the market before dawn
to buy fish, vegetables, and fruit and invited Emilie to
have lunch with them at the Parisian. Emilie could
hardly believe it. She said: "If it weren't just a weak-
ness of age, I'd swear there are no more inflexible men
left on the face of the earth." But there were at least
two, because those two sons of hers spit insults at the
mere mention of their sister's name. And you want to
know why? It was because of the looks they got—
wherever they went, walking down the street, in their
favorite clubs and bars, people looked at them, reti-
cently or openly, and the looks on their faces demand-
ed the particulars, they were unsatisfied with the
stories going around from mouth to mouth transforming an event into a web of contradictory suppositions.
After your grandfather died, they went to even greater
lengths. They sent Samara threatening letters, they
telephoned in the middle of the night to call her dirty
names, and once they hired a couple of kids to throw
rocks through her bedroom window.

The only thing that kept them from actually physically assaulting her was the fact that Emilie controlled
the Parisian's cash box and guarded the money in the
English safe whose combination was known only to
her. It was precisely this secret that put food on their
families' tables; all the more reason, since it was a
matter of life or death, for the secret of the safe to re-
strain them in their moments of greatest fury against

Samara Délia. Living alone in that house, without a husband, or servants, or anyone, just the animals, the statues on the fountain, the plants and flowers, expressing her thanks through protests to the condescending neighbors who made a point of looking in on her daily (and to the Commander, who offered her the company of the family's live-in French tutor, who spent days and nights in total idleness), Emilie's main concern was not fear of a solitary death but the security of that safe, since she knew that when she died those sons of hers would take possession of the house and the Parisian by force and Samara would be thrown out into the street without a penny. Yes, that's right, she revealed to me—and I believe only to me—the secret of the safe, which she had carried off and hidden in an unlikely place as soon as she realized her husband was nearing the end.

One Sunday night around that time she took me by the arm and said, "Come with me." She had a flashlight with her, though it was turned off; we crossed the dark patio and yard very carefully so as not to wake the animals, and when we came to the chicken coop she took the key off the handle of the flashlight and unlocked the door. The chickens didn't stir or scratch the ground, maybe because they were used to your grandmother's nocturnal visits; anyway, she walked a few steps to the pigeon house back behind the last roost, squatted down, and began feeling around in the damp earth that reeked of chicken manure. Only then did she turn on the flashlight and shine it on the ground, and found an overturned gourd set into the dung. "The keys are in here," said Emilie, picking up the gourd. One key opened the wooden door to the pigeon house, and inside was an enormous metal box, with a green door and five dials, the alphabet inscribed around them, and four more with numbers from zero to nine. She turned the red spot on each dial to the successive letters and numbers of the secret code, so that they read clockwise: AMLAS, 1881. Then she turned the key, pressed the knob, opened the metal door, and shone the flashlight into the inside of the safe.

"Here are my riches," she exclaimed, running her fingers over a Bible, a couple of photo albums, letters, and sundry papers. There were little metal drawers where she kept the money from the Parisian that Samara brought her every weekend. Every corner of the strongbox was crammed with stuff, but Emilie focused the light, and then her voice, on the confusion: "Here are the children's baby albums, there are the pictures of Chipre and Marseilles from our voyage to Brazil, and that little box is full of letters from Sister Virginie." Pressed between the pages of the Old Testament like a religious relic were the dry petals of an orchid that a homeless, diseased beggar gave her the day Emir disappeared. By way of thanks, she had presented the poor, wretched man with some gifts as valuable to him as the orchid was to her: a lamb, a sack of manioc meal, a large can of olive oil, and two male pigeons, and she advised him to talk to a lay brother or priest. The petals had yellowed like the wedding picture she slipped from the Bible with trembling hands. Then she showed me some jewelry from our homeland and explained that she wore it only for special parties and receptions, and also for moments of reconciliation with her husband. At that point she furrowed her brow and turned her face away, maybe at the thought of her husband suffering in his room; but even so she didn't cry. I asked her once why she never cried to ease her worldly sorrows, and she told me that only death brings relief: "That's when the body and the soul finally decide to agree and enjoy the silence of eternity," she said without blinking.

Squatting there in the chicken coop that night, as Emilie went on showing me things from the past, I got upset thinking about your grandfather moaning alone in his room, unable to recognize familiar faces. At least he had come to the end of his life as he'd always wanted to, living by himself, with no witnesses and at a distance from everything: from the hate, the jealousy, the hope, and the dread. Emilie noticed my uneasiness and immediately began returning things to their places; then she closed the door of the safe, spun the dials, and asked me to open it again. On the third try I got it. We tiptoed back across the patio, careful once more not to wake the animals. In the pantry, she showed me where she hid the flashlight and the key to the chicken coop: inside an old porcelain water filter, exactly like the kind English sailors used to sell. Then she offered me some garlic water and drank a whole pitcher herself before going upstairs to pray at her

husband's bedside. I never had to open the safe, because the scenario Emilie most feared, with her wild
sons acting their nastiest and destroying Samara
Délia, never occurred. What did happen was what
Emilie least expected, and it was one more blow in her
life. After her father's death, Samara took charge of
the Parisian all by herself and put such energy into the
store that within a few years Emilie had to mock her
dead husband:

"In five years that store has made more than it did in
fifty with him in charge! He was better at sermonizing
from a minaret than at standing quietly behind the
counter."

In any case, Emilie and Samara continued as they
were: Emilie in the house, with the animals, receiving
sporadic visits, and seeing her sons once a month or
less. Samara Délia working, eating, and sleeping alone
in the Parisian, visiting her mother once a week, always quiet as a mouse, thinking who knows what.
Samara had always been striking, and it seemed as if
time and mourning had made her even more beautiful. The last time I saw her she was dressed all in
black. It was a Sunday morning at Emilie's house,
with a group of neighbors gathered around the fountain, talking. Emilie decided to open the bird cages
and free the birds, even the rarest ones, convinced this
gesture would give her the heart to live peacefully for
a little longer. "From now on, I only want free animals
in this house," she said for all to hear as the birds
flapped around us. A few of them remained in their

open cages, waiting for birdseed, a piece of banana, and a face every morning imitating their songs as it approached the metal cage. Instead of forcing them to fly away, she just said: "These birds are part of me. We'll fly away together, God only knows when and where." Samara helped her mother clean out the rest of the cages, throwing pieces of leftover French toast and other table scraps to the fish and alligators, and walked under the fruit trees with a pitcher of genipap nectar, filling the glass flowers and vials that hung on the branches among the leaves.

There were two things jarringly different about Samara that morning. She was the picture of elegance in high-heeled shoes, expensive silk stockings, and a wide-brimmed Italian straw hat shading the mother-of-pearl scarab on the yoke of her black cotton dress; the guests' jaws dropped and your grandmother beamed with pride, though she did think the outfit a bit austere for a Sunday morning and asked if Samara were planning to go to ten o'clock mass. Samara smiled and gave Emilie that oblique look of hers. Then she joined in on the conversation, which was an amazement to everyone because she was usually extremely quiet in front of people. That day she talked animatedly about this and that, remarking on local events, new faces at the Parisian, which customers ran up a tab and which paid cash; she talked about how the saplings her father had planted were blooming now and bearing fruit; she asked Arminda if Esmeralda liked living in Rio de Janeiro; she asked Yasmine if her husband was still struggling to raise silkworms in this infernal climate; she asked Mentaha if she still had the crazy habit of hunting gray pigeons in the middle of the night for special weekend meals; and then she turned to me and asked if I still lived all alone in the old house on the other side of Emilie's backyard. I said yes, that it was an ideal place to live for an old single woman without a family. And once again she smiled, as she handed her mother a zippered bag. Emilie told me later that the bag had contained some money, a thick leather-bound book, a letter, and a few other things she didn't want to talk about. Till the end of her days she regretted not having opened that bag the minute it was handed to her. "But at just that moment the bells began ringing ten o'clock, and I didn't want her to be late for mass just to give me a sales report," she told me. That night, when Emilie took the bag out back to the safe, she made such a hullabaloo that I ran to my porch to see what was going on. There she was, sitting limply on the edge of the stone seashell, one hand resting on an angel's leg and the other petting a sheep's head. The patio lights were on, so I could see the fish roiling the water, and a lot of the animals were still shrieking up a storm, but your grandmother looked oblivious to it all. I didn't want to call to her, so I just sat trying to figure out why she was sitting there frozen between the angel and the animal. I was sitting in this very chair, and I know I dozed off once in a while but every time I opened my eyes there she was in the exact same position; then I remembered something your grandfather said one night when Emilie suddenly pointed at Amadou Tifachi and everybody stopped talking. Amadou was a North African poet, a friend of Dorner's, who was visiting Amazonas. He'd been telling wild stories all evening, all kinds of obscene episodes and exchanges, tales of shameless lovers, and of licentious lips that, according to him, wandered from men's faces to women's lower parts. And that jerk had the nerve to call himself a writer and a religious person. It's true that everyone was laughing, and the women were in stitches, dying of shame, because of the way he used his hands as well as his tongue to talk. He went on for so long and so energetically that by the end of the night he left the circle to drink an entire pitcher of tamarind juice and devour a potful of beef and lentils. It was almost dawn when Emilie pointed over toward the fountain, and there he was, motionless, all in white, like a plaster saint. That was when your grandfather said: "Anytime anyone stays quiet for a good long stretch, if he's not sleeping he's got to be contemplating love or death."

Emilie was clearly not sleeping. The next morning I found out what had happened. Samara Délia had left without much fuss, just a quick see-you-later. All the same, when she walked away there had been a stupefied silence, a sense of mystery, shared even by the animals. I think all of us wanted to say something about it, but we didn't; for some unknown reason, we just couldn't manage to say a word. Emilie gazed thought-

fully at the few cages with birds still in them, Mentaha pressed her fingers to her temples to relieve her
eternal migraine, Yasmine stood with her eyes closed,
breathing in the morning air, and Arminda's ever-
smiling face was turned down toward the hands in her
lap, which were embroidering the Commander's initials on a satin handkerchief. I was thinking about
Samara. After certain events, even the most unexpected and unforeseeable, we can't help lamenting the fact
that we aren't clairvoyant, or at least capable of a tiny
drop of premonition, just enough to prevent something undesirable from happening. When I arrived
that Monday morning Emilie was tense and flustered,
and I found out that it was too late to prevent one of
those unhappy events. Something in the bag Samara
had given her led her to believe that Samara was gone
for good, and Emilie had been stewing about it all
night. A number of regular customers had called to try
to find out why the store was locked up tight. When
Emilie walked over there she found everything in perfect order, and the only things missing from Samara's
room were some clothes and the framed picture of Soraya. Emilie rented out the Parisian that very week
and sold all the merchandise to the tenant. All she
carried away was several pieces of fabric and two or
three boxes of bridal veils that had been left in the
storeroom. She announced that there are certain
goods that time transforms into objects of value to us,
and for this reason some hand-painted Spanish fans
had been kept off the showcase shelves because they

were similar to the ones her husband gave her the night they became engaged. And so Emilie filled her bedroom with objects that commemorated an important event in her life and decided never even to walk past the Parisian until Samara Délia reappeared. But meanwhile she didn't so much as mention the idea of searching for her daughter; she actually refused offers of help from half the world—above all, Uncle Emílio, who eagerly volunteered to scour the city and even the country in search of his niece. The last time she had searched for someone, Emilie remembered, it had ended in disaster: if Emir had been allowed to stay with that prostitute in Marseilles, maybe he'd still be alive today. She declared the subject closed, claiming it would be a waste of time to wander the city looking for her daughter, because Samara was headstrong, stubborn, and proud.

"Maybe she'll be less unhappy that way, living in anonymity in an unknown city, where no one knows about her past," said Emilie.

The last few years Emilie had suffered like a penitent, just to keep family disasters from coming up in conversation. So she invented remodeling projects, weeded the garden, pruned the vines and trees, and shined the mirrors and windows until they sparkled. One morning I found her sitting beside the outside washtub scrubbing Sálua's shell with a steel brush and applying beeswax to the cracks and scrapes caused by collisions with the other animals and the perverse games of children, grandchildren, and stepchildren;

then she buffed his shell with a resin-soaked flannel cloth and finally set him back down on the little sand beach in front of the small pond filled with dozens of his children. Without looking up she exclaimed, "Sálua is my living mirror." She also invented various ailments that appeared in the morning and disappeared before nightfall, and spent two years swearing and complaining that a callus on the sole of her right foot was developing into gangrene, leaving her crippled and unable to satisfy her irresistible desire to wander the house from five A.M. until sleep finally came to her. Last year sometime, I don't for the life of me know why, Emilie became convinced that Samara's return depended entirely on those undependable sons of hers. She got herself all worked up and insisted that they both make a public declaration promising a definitive reconciliation. Emílio and I managed to persuade her to give up this silly idea, which made sense only as a clear indication of the depth of her despair. Even so, she insisted on trying to convince them to reconnect with their sister. She told each of them separately that rancor corrodes a man, and that even as she neared the end of her life she still hadn't managed to understand the hatred they felt, much less its endurance over the years. The first one just sneered at what she said and the second spat out an indictment that had been tormenting her something awful these last days: "Mama, you gave birth to a whore; you should hate her, too, and understand better than anyone how we feel."

Emilie's reaction seemed calm, almost apathetic, at

first. She listened impassively to what he said, her eyes on his; he simply sat there in the living room, his back to the clock on the wall. Emilie did not take her eyes off him, even when, with a mixture of astonishment and confusion, he stood up and left, as if he were running away from danger or from something that was eating at him from the inside. The strangest thing was that Emilie didn't even blink, and I was scared of that look in her eyes that seemed to see no one and nothing. I thought it even stranger that when I walked up to her it was as if a shadow slid across the living-room mirror, or as if I were still hiding in the leaves outside the window, spying on mother and son as they talked. I had to plop down right in front of her to get her attention. And then, still staring into space, she muttered: "I'm fine, alone like this."

That was Friday, a week before she died. It was her last encounter with her son and maybe with life itself. The following week she hardly slept, but still she dreamed, a lot.

"The little I sleep is to dream," she told me last Sunday as she rummaged through the moldy things in a trunk, stacking up old photographs and letters. Those last days we sat around on the patio several times and talked. She remembered the name of a plant and remarked: "Anastácia planted that one, and that trellis over there was a gift from one of the maids who quit because she was afraid of my boys." She talked about your Uncle Hakim, who became a man without her ever seeing his man's face, since he left Manaus at just over twenty. Of course, he sent photos and letters, but she'd have given everything he sent for one quick look in his eyes. She showed me a picture: "Doesn't he look exactly like Emirzinho?" And, halfway between sheepish and distressed, she answered her own question: "My first son and my little brother. Two pearls from the same necklace." Emilie never complained of being tired, but there were dark circles under her eyes, and her fine features had begun to dissolve. She seemed to be busier than ever, and through the night she hardly missed a tolling of the bells. I think all those sleepless nights were what made her lightheaded.

Over the final three days, Tuesday through Thursday, Emilie reported a flood of dreams in which Emir and Hakim always appeared. She asked me to read to her from Hakim's letters while she gazed at pictures of both of them in the album open on her lap. Hakim, who had gone to live in the south, did look a lot like Emir, who had died while still a young man. As she looked at their photographs side by side, the likeness began to bother her: they seemed to be smiling the same smile. Referring to her dreams, she said dreamily: "All those times we were together, the three of us sailing a boat downriver to meet the sea." And all the dreams she recounted seemed to be the same one, and she always sat gazing at the pictures, and then she'd say: "Read to me, Hindié, read to me from Hakim's letters." On Thursday she seemed to be feeling good, walking back and forth and around the fountain, pausing to watch the fish, at peace with herself, quiet, as if she'd accepted the idea that something was ending. The only sound her body made as she moved was the tinkling of the four golden bracelets on her left wrist. Everything in the house was spotless, nothing, not a single object, out of place.

EPILOGUE

INDIÉ FALLS SILENT all of a sudden, and sadness slowly fills her eyes. From her porch, she contemplates the view of the crown of the jambo tree across the yard and the bedroom windows of Emilie's house, closed forever. The distance between the two houses grows smaller under her gaze, and, in the silence of her eyes, memory is doing its work. No more dramatic gestures, no fervent hugs and kisses; she just surrenders to the almost silent weeping that somehow seems to carry on its own communion with the jagged, sun-drenched landscape, equally silent, but lacking eyes or memory. The house is closed and deserted; before long the slate patio will be coated with mold; vines will eventually cover window shutters, railings, jalousies, and close all the gaps through which eyes can follow the course of the sun and perceive the invasion of night, sudden and dense. Hindié's eyes seem to be communing with something very like night, with objects abandoned in the dark, with the slow footsteps that people a house, a world: the two patios, the fountain spilling its water, the flora joining earth and sky, and the animals who are strangers to confinement and become excited at the sound of Emilie's voice.

Sunday morning draws to an end, nothing happens, Hindié's face remains mute, the agitation of body and speech of earlier seems to have passed; maybe she's reflecting on her loss. In the solitude of old age people feed on absences, there are so many truths to be forgotten and a fountain of myths that can become truths in their place. Sometimes I imagine Hindié alone, roaming the diminutive, almost nonexistent border that separates death from night, memory from death. I picture her also in the silence of that Sunday, her eyes fixed on the landscape framed before her: half a tree and part of a house—the closed plane of a facade without shadows under the sun that splits the day.

EARLY FRIDAY AFTERNOON Yasmine called to tell me that friends and relatives were still gathered at the house; Uncle Hakim was due to arrive any minute, and Uncle Emílio and the neighbors had made all the funeral arrangements. This news sounded like a summons. I was expected to attend the farewell to Emilie: first the mass, with the body present, the Archbishop of Manaus officiating, and then a coffee hour at the house at three P.M. I decided not to go until these proceedings were over, all the unpleasantness of the goodbyes, but I still arrived in time to watch the funeral procession. The sons headed up the cortege, and Emilie's three women friends rented cars so some of the frequent visitors to the house could come along, humble folk whom Emilie had helped as much as she could, giving them leftover food, old clothes, sometimes even finding them odd jobs at somebody's house. Or inviting the ones who couldn't remember when they last had something to eat to stop by for a sandwich. Sometimes when local delinquents or unemployed people were picked up by soldiers or worried homeowners for roaming the neighborhood trying to smell out uninhabited houses, they'd send her notes full of such pleading and repentance that she'd go to the barracks personally to try to convince the commanding officer to free the detainees, insisting that they, too, were children of God and not mad dogs. With a verbal blast that was almost unintelligible but at the same time extremely moving, she managed to get them released and, on top of that, in front of everyone, delivered a gentle scolding and sermon just as a mother does with rebellious children.

The other members of the funeral procession were relatives of the Commander and Esmeralda, who had herself left Manaus after her husband died. The women of both families were still in mourning, and the black veils covering their faces seemed to refer to Emilie's death and to so many others that have taken place here and overseas, as if the death of one friend awakens an interminable succession of memories of all those we've been close to. Maybe that's why we're not sure, wrapped up in our grief and regret, whether it's born of yesterday's loss or one that took place a long time ago, a long line of lifeless bodies resurfacing with great intensity in our memories, widening its melancholy horizon.

I tried to watch people's faces as the procession made its way from the square to the cemetery. I stayed in the car, preferring to remain on the fringes. The last phase of that exhausting afternoon took place at Emilie's, where we found Uncle Hakim standing still as a statue under the dark crown of the jambo tree.

The next day I returned to the cemetery to visit Emilie's grave and ran into Adamor Piedade, who was his quiet self, like a shadow stirring in the serene Saturday morning air that contained neither rain nor heat, laughter nor lamentations. He recognized me immediately, because the day before he'd waved to me from a distance; someone had told him I was Soraya Ângela's cousin, the child who had cried in sorrow at her death. We talked awhile in the cool shade of the mango trees, where you used to go scouting for fruit and tried to scale the white slabs that are meant to immortalize what is already dust. Adamor told me a little about his life, altogether dedicated to digging holes to shelter the dead; he told me about the city's famous dead and its barefoot dead, buried any which where, without cherubim or celestial music, with no illusion of a future life. He complained of a perpetual migraine, terrible back pain, galloping fatigue, and the arduous, tedious, colorless, monotonous all-day-long. What did this man who had buried thousands think of death? He said the city had grown a lot in the last years, because he was working like a dog.

"Death didn't used to be so trivial," he said. "It meant something. A burial was a noteworthy event; someone was born and there were celebrations; someone closed his eyes for the last time and everything turned ceremonial, and elegant. This multitude of marble and stone among the trees keeps me company, and the living who come here don't talk so much as they cry. I've gotten used to this life surrounded by silent neighbors. . . ."

But just before dawn this morning he'd been startled by a solemn voice, neither soft nor loud, alternating between melody and lament and now and then interrupted suddenly by a brief quietness, a breath of silence. "I've heard all kinds of litanies and prayers," said Adamor, "but this one was different from all the others." He walked out to meet the voice and finally saw a figure beside the family gravesite. In addition to the oddness of the song, the position of the body intrigued him: neither kneeling nor lying down, but kind of crouched over forward, with both arms outstretched to the first rays of the rising sun.

"I kept an eye out, waiting for the first little threads of dawn," Adamor went on, "to get a glimpse of the face. And I didn't get more than a glimpse, either, because the person's head seemed to be aiming for the ground, trying to dive into the end of night and disappear. I didn't realize until later that it wasn't your Uncle Hakim's voice I'd heard but a black box he'd placed on top of your grandfather's grave. Well, I'll tell you, I crossed myself so fast, as most people do who walk past that grave and don't know what to think because there's no cross, no floral wreath, no saint's image, not a single sign of Christian burial. Never mind that voiceless body murmuring, his back to the grave. . . ."

Adamor wanted to know why, so many whys: why that strange prayer, why the odd position alone on the ground, the throaty, metallic voice, trying to be song and speech and prayer all at once.

I myself resisted the idea of a body in Manaus turned toward Mecca, as if the space belief requires were as vast as the universe: a body bends toward a temple, an oracle, a statue, or a figure, and all geography disappears or converges with the black stone sleeping inside each of us.

IN YOUR NEXT-TO-LAST letter you wondered when I was planning to leave the hospital and, "not meaning to be indiscreet," wondered a whole lot of other things, too. Then you quipped: "Don't take this as an epistolary inquisition." Of course I didn't, but your extravagant curiosity does take me by surprise sometimes, leaving me puzzled and disarmed. What was it like living at the hospital? Well, I spent the first few weeks submerged in the serene darkness of continuous, dreamless sleep. It was as if I were blindfolded, as if sudden and premature blindness were a defense against Mother's arrival. She came as soon as she heard I had been hospitalized. I don't think I ever really saw her, not even from a distance. But one night, when I looked out the open door of my room, I thought I saw a vague shape in the shadows, as if someone had fled the bright light to hide in the dim region between the threshold and the edge of the world. Maybe it was her, because I remember hearing the voice that abandoned us so long ago. The voice was talking to Emilie, reaching out from a distant place, news of our lives. That body and that voice, which had seemed so close to me, became no more than a pale memory of an imaginary encounter; and they vanished altogether once I emerged from my state of sluggishness to enter the highly organized, antiseptic, and sober space around me, where I was constantly buffeted by the hallucinatory din that patients made before being returned to the lethargic sleep of new arrivals who checked in to spend days on end relieved of any lucid or creative gesture whatsoever, as if sleeping at the bottom of the ocean, doing nothing but breathing beside the sea monsters and poisonous seaweed that hover between the muddy depths and the surface high above.

Days passed as I sat wondering how I managed to end up there and expecting my friend to confirm my worst fear, which was already a certainty, since deep down I knew that I'd been hospitalized on Mother's orders after my last outburst of wild fury, when nothing in my house had been left standing or whole or in its place. I came without offering much resistance, like a blind person or a lost child being led to a familiar place. And there, just a few kilometers from town, madness and solitude were my familiars. I'd look out my window at the tangle of tall, gray buildings disappearing and reemerging and think that out there (where the masses are crammed into apartments or in shacks made of planks and scraps of cardboard) there was also enough madness and solitude to go around. I spent some time studying the panorama of the city and the patio at the "rest clinic," with its concrete benches, grassy paths, and trees. Before the afternoon was over I'd leave my room to watch the women who came to venerate twilight or find a respite from despair and loneliness. Some of them told the same stories over and over, invoking the past to keep it alive, and to redeem the origin of everything (a life, a place, a time). There was the woman in black who would take off her clothes and run back to her room and then suddenly appear again dressed in black and lie down under a tree, where she remained, leaning against the trunk, until she disappeared, blending into the night. There was a couple who danced to an imaginary song, and also a woman with green eyes, known as Beautiful Maria Ares, who would walk slowly up to anyone who let her and pull out a picture of a man and show it with the devotion of someone displaying a saint's image or a martyr's. Once in a while I'd hear the shouting from the other side of the wall and remember that there was more to the place than just our enclosed space, and that it wasn't time or space or night that separated the women's wing from the men's but a solid, insurmountable wall. After gazing at the picture in her hand, Beautiful Maria Ares would point to the wall; once she'd tried to scale it by digging the tips of her fingers into the cracks between the stones, but was caught and isolated from the rest of us for a while as punishment. The men's wing, on the other side of the building, seemed more inaccessible and distant to us than the city. The hospital's design resembled a butterfly: the body contained the rooms, the head the administration, and the two symmetrical wings encompassed patios, dining halls, and gardens, with grass and stone paths winding through the trees and enclosed by iron gates.

Sometimes my friend Miriam would visit, and I'd tell her about day-to-day occurrences, conversations with doctors, and the reports they wrote after observing my gestures, my expression, and the people I talked to. My daily life was rigorously cataloged and scheduled down to the last detail. In order to amuse myself, to distort the truth a little, and to make representation into something intriguing, I made up dreams and imaginary incidents to tell the doctors. I never invented anything about our parents, but I didn't talk much about them anyway. The doctors listened with a cold patience that underlined their lack of emotion. These sessions were conducted by people dressed all in white and took place in a room with white walls situated at the tip of the butterfly's head; it was a bit like being in an aquarium full of dead fish, which was a striking contrast to the clamor on the patio: the realm of emotion and the savage state of desire. Miriam brought me books, letters, needle and thread, and news of the outside. She heard that Mother was going to Europe and would stop in Barcelona to see you. My own story with her is the story of the failure to connect. I realize this ticklish subject doesn't much appeal to you. "I feel like I'm walking on eggshells," you'd say whenever I brought it up. The very topic burns, words of fire, the Devil's conversation, right? I know you lived with her for a little while, but I left Manaus before you did and saw her only once when I was a child. Emilie never kept the truth from me; she was completely open: "Your mother is an impossible presence," she'd say. "She's the stranger caught in the other side of the mirror." Miriam thought it was strange that I didn't leave the hospital sooner than I did. It bothered her to sit on the patio, and she'd shudder whenever those two religious ladies would walk over with their eyes wide and kneel down in front of us, clutching their transparent rosary beads. "What is it about this place that makes you want to stay here?" she asked me. I wanted to ask back: What is it about the outside world that should make me want to be out there? But instead I just told her I was thinking about taking a trip.

I spent my time at the clinic either on the patio with the others or in my room at my window, which opened on two worlds. In the distance, behind the foul air and dizzying movement of the city that was expanding by the minute, lay the world of confusion. Torn apart by the difficult pursuit of ephemeral pleasures, such as the delicate imprint of a spiral shell on the sand, soon to be washed away by the waves, I still bore scars from that world: my despair and my impatience to survive. The other, all-too-visible world pulsed just a few steps from my window. After two weeks at the clinic I could identify the voice of each person with my eyes closed, as well as picture the gestures of those who never spoke and hear the prayers of those who prayed out loud. My room was a privileged place of solitude where I learned to do needlework. I cut up an old sheet to make some handkerchiefs, on which I embroidered people's initials or nicknames, or abstract designs for those squares I planned to give people who didn't have or weren't known by their names, people who never looked at me, never looked at themselves: bodies without speech, excluded from the conversation, who seemed to be walking in a desert with no God and no oasis, leaving behind a trail erased by the wind and the hot breath of death.

Sometimes at night, especially when I lay awake with insomnia, I'd risk traveling here or there; all my trips were imaginary, travels into memory. Sometimes I'd hungrily read and reread your letters, including some very old ones from when you were still in Madrid, and you complained many times of my silence or my delay in writing back. Around that time, during roughly the last week of my time in the hospital, I wrote a kind of report. I wouldn't know whether to call it a story, a novel, or a fable, just words and phrases with no pretension to any genre or literary form. I did try to find a theme to focus the narrative, but each sentence evoked a different topic, an image distinct from the one before, and everything got all jumbled together on each page: fragments from your letters and my diary, a description of my arrival in São Paulo, an old dream dredged up from memory, the murder of a nun, the commotion of downtown Manaus, a tempest of a hailstorm, a flower crumpled in a child's hand, and the voice of a woman who never once said my name out loud. I thought about sending you a copy, but then I tore it up without really knowing why and made a collage with the scraps. I glued some of the hankies embroidered with abstract shapes in among the texture of letters and words; I liked the mix of paper and cloth, colorful thread, black ink, and white paper. The overall shape wasn't meant to be representative of anything, but if you looked at it carefully you might begin to see a crude face. Yes, a face, shapeless or fragmented, maybe the first intimation of my sudden desire to travel to Manaus after such a long absence. I knew I didn't want to arrive in daylight, I wanted to avoid the surprises that can come with brightness and clarity and instead return blind, like certain birds who shelter in the dark crowns of solitary trees, or a body that flees a ball of fire to dive into the tempestuous sea of memory.

To a traveler looking out the plane window at night,

it seems as if a river of stories is flowing into an invisible city. Flying above the dark jungle for hours, you search for a sign of life down below, but there's not a single luminous speck to be found. No fanfare announces the end of the long flight; suddenly, like the lights of a gigantic ship on an ocean separating two continents, a terrestrial and aquatic constellation of lights tells you that the forest below is changing its name, that the river, invisible before, has turned into a brightly lit path, and even its banks and tributaries and tributaries of tributaries, even the forest, sparkles with scattered points of light. This diffuse brightness makes you think that the city, the river, and the jungle light up at the same time and are inseparable, and that the plane, navigating the equator, is splitting open two incandescent lobes. Even as you lose altitude, aware of the changing angle of vision and the fact that only eight or ten thousand meters are between you and the ground, there is nothing to help you distinguish asphalt roads from riverways from dense jungle: a sinuous trail of light could be a boat or a car, and the fixed and brilliant lights concentrated in one area might be a street, a port, a town square, or a whole neighborhood emerging from the water.

It was after eleven o'clock when I stood in front of the unfamiliar house beside Emilie's. I hadn't let anyone know I was arriving that night, but I knew that since Mother wasn't there the maid would be alone. I walked along the house to the back and through a breezeway leading from the back door through a huge garden to the rear part of the yard. It was very dark out by the servants' quarters. A single bulb cast some light on the garden. Instead of waking the maid, I decided to spend the night in the open air, lying on the grass or sitting in one of the chairs scattered about under the jambo trees or the palm trees that rose above the roofline. I hadn't brought much with me: a valise with some clothes and a small photograph album full of pictures taken at Emilie's, the sphere of my childhood. I hadn't forgotten my diary, of course, and at the last minute I also decided to bring my tape recorder, some tapes, and all your letters. In the most recent one, after hearing that I was coming to Manaus, you asked me to write down everything I could: "Especially if something unexpected should happen while you're there, examine all the facts, like a good reporter, or an anatomy student, or Stubb, the dissector of whales."

That turned out to involve a lot of work. I made several tapes and filled a dozen notebooks with observations, but I never felt up to putting things in order. My attempts were innumerable and exhaustive, but by the time I would reach the end of a story someone told me or a passage describing an event, I'd find that everything had gotten mixed up in a disconnected constellation of episodes, with rumors from all quarters, irrelevant facts, and numerous dates and figures sticking out all over. Whenever I managed to link the voices or to impose some organization on the jumble of episodes, some gap would yawn where forgetfulness and hesitancy lived: the dead space that undermines the consecutiveness of ideas. And this allowed me to jettison the important, perhaps imperative, task of organizing my account so I wouldn't leave it hanging, drifting with the wind, structured by chance. Looking at the immensity of the river that drinks large gulps of rain forest as it flows by, I thought of someone lost in his meanderings, paddling in search of a tributary that would lead to the main branch, or to the glimmer of a port in the distance. I felt like that person on the river, constantly moving but lost in the movement, goaded on by a tenacious will to escape: motion that leads to still more confused waters following their uncertain courses.

How many times I started over again organizing the episodes, and how many times I was surprised to run afoul of the same beginning, or the dizzying back-and-forth of interlinking chapters made up of pages and pages numbered in a chaotic way. Then I stumbled on another problem: how to transcribe the mumbling of some and the foreign accents of others? So many shared confidences from different people in so few days echoed like a chorus of dispersed voices. All that remained was to use my own voice, gliding like a huge, fragile bird over the other voices. So the recorded statements, the narration of events, everything audible and visible that I had to report came to be guided by a single voice struggling between hesitation and the murmurs of the past. And the past itself was like an invisible pursuer, a transparent, beckoning hand, leading me toward times and places a great distance from my brief stay in Manaus. Groping for a way to reveal (in a letter that would be the abbreviated compilation of a life) that Emilie was gone forever, I tried to use the eyes of memory to recall events from our childhood, lines of poetry, special feasts, the way people talked, our peals of laughter at the hybrid language Emilie invented every day of her life.

It was as if I were trying to whisper to you the melody of a fugitive music, and little by little scattered notes and cadences began to rephrase the lost song.